Previous Works

It Must Be Tuesday
Copyright © 2016 Art Hanford Jr
Reg. # TXu 1-999-803
April 1, 2016

Who Cares About Danny?
Copyright © 2008 Kelly Danten, a Pseudonym
Reg. # TX7-128-149
April 25, 2008

My Bodeskabreau
Copyright © 2010 Art Hanford Jr.
Reg # TX7-340-555
June 3, 2010

The Westerville Solution
A Trilogy:
The Stain
Copyright © 2013 Art Hanford Jr.
Reg # TXu-1-863-456
March 11, 2013
The Secret Oasis
Copyright © 2013 Art Hanford Jr.
Reg # TXu-1924-229
October 12, 2013
The Dead End
Copyright © 2013 Art Hanford Jr.
Reg # TXu-1-893-000

WIDOWS
OF THE
WESTERN RESERVE

ART HANFORD JR.

 iUniverse®

WIDOWS OF THE WESTERN RESERVE

iUniverse books may be ordered through booksellers or by contacting:

iUniverse
1663 Liberty Drive
Bloomington, IN 47403
www.iuniverse.com
1-800-Authors (1-800-288-4677)

Because of the dynamic nature of the Internet, any web addresses or
links contained in this book may have changed since publication and
may no longer be valid. The views expressed in this work are solely those
of the author and do not necessarily reflect the views of the publisher,
and the publisher hereby disclaims any responsibility for them.

Any people depicted in stock imagery provided by Getty Images are
models, and such images are being used for illustrative purposes only.
Certain stock imagery © Getty Images.

ISBN: 978-1-5320-4216-4 (sc)
ISBN: 978-1-5320-4217-1 (e)

Library of Congress Control Number: 2018902631

Print information available on the last page.

iUniverse rev. date: 03/24/2018

Characters in Widows of the Western Reserve

HELEN AND TERESA____SISTERS....Daughters of Art Donley

TAYLOR_____HELEN'S GRANDDAUGHTER...TERESA'S NIECE

HELEN _____Widow of Henry Beck; mother of Howard Beck; Taylor's grandmother; mother-in-law to Cynthia,

TERESA____ Widow of John Townsend: Taylor's great aunt; Helen's sister; died in 2017; mother of Philip Townsend

TAYLOR____Taylor Beck, 15-year-old daughter of widowed daughter-in-law Cynthia Beck ;Teresa's "niece"......

Helen's granddaughter

JOHN TOWNSEND__ Teresa's deceased veteran husband Taylor's great uncle died in the 1970s

PHILIP TOWNSEND___Son of John and Teresa

BILL TOWNSEND____Teresa's grandson...son of Phillip

DEDICATION

To all the widows who struggled against discrimination to establish a home and help build communities deep in the wilderness of the Western Reserve. It is also to recognize authors Edwin Hall, Henry Ellsworth, Gertrude Rensselaer, Harlan Hatcher. Harvey Rice, Rev. William Hanford, Augustus G. Goldings, Shieley M.De Boer, Harriet Beecher Stowe and Harriet Taylor Upton for their published descriptions of what it was like in those early years of our country. This is also to recognize and thank individuals and organizations who provided information that helped put it all together, including the Western Reserve Historical Society, the Veterans Administration and some sources on the internet. Mostly, it is to thank my wife Janice for her patience and understanding; my son Guy, for providing material and ideas for the book; my son-in-law Ron for his valuable suggestions; and to apologize if I misspelled anybody's name.

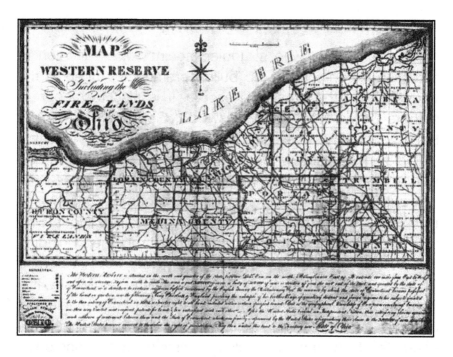

Drawing of "Western Reserve, including Fire Lands of Ohio" courtesy of David Rumsey Map Collection...www.davidrumsey.com

PROLOGUE

It is common to hear about the troubles many settlers had during the early days of the Western Reserve--travel was difficult, food was scarce. Danger from foreign soldiers and savage Indians lurked in the lush forests. It is difficult to compare those troubles with the hardships facing either parent left alone in that hostile environment.

Widows--and widowers--are seldom mentioned in accounts of the Western Reserves' development in the 1800s. Hundreds of books, diaries, church records, military and county records, reveal details of wealthy survivors--usually male descendants. They give little attention to their widows--and their families-- now left alone.

What became of those widows? Who were they? What did they accomplish?

With the aid of the National Register, the Western Reserve Historical Society and a lot of research, we hope to correct this oversight by matching widows' names with men who died in the Revolutionary War, the War of 1812, the countless skirmishes with Indians and the devastating diseases rampant in that period of our history.

We found stories about the widows who helped settle towns, who ran the grist mills, retrieved salt from salt springs, taught in schools, ran for office, saved lives, wrote diaries, fought slavery, led religious groups and encouraged charitable acts for their neighbors.

First, we need to review details about the Western Reserve: What is it? Where is it? When did it start? Who is responsible? Who were the Windows of the Western Reserve?

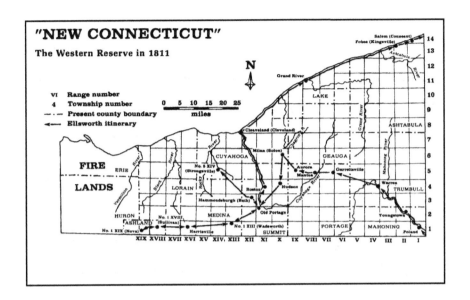

Map of "New Connecticut...The Western Reserve in 1811" courtesy of Western Reserve Historical Society, the archival repository.

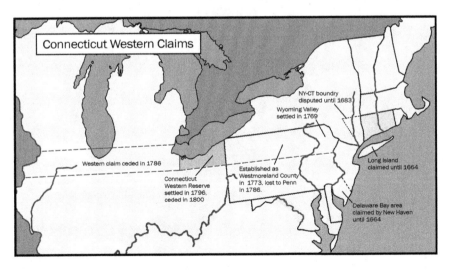

CONTENTS

CHAPTER I

THE CURIOUS COUSIN

Helen was often asked by her daughter-in-law to babysit her granddaughter, a teen-ager who was growing like a weed. She said she enjoyed doing it, especially when it gave her an opportunity to spend time with Taylor, a fifteen year-old high school student with the looks and ambition to be a Hollywood film star.

The youngster had the run of the house. She had her own room with a closet full of clothes. She had a pile of CD's with music she enjoyed. The pantry was full of snacks.

They could talk about anything that was on their mind, including boyfriends and prospects she was eyeing for a future husband. "Gramma" she would ask, "How do you know when you have picked the right guy?"

Helen...from her favorite position snuggled on a couch... answered slowly "Not as easy as you might think ... much of the time, it's the guy who picks the girl...give it a rest...you have plenty of time."

"What could they look for?" persisted the granddaughter, who was eager to get out of her school uniform.

"Well, they might want to know about you, your family, where your ancestors came from, health records, their financial situation, their religion, their politics, maybe nothing," Helen replied.

"I don't know the first thing about my ancestors," bellowed the teen-ager...and I won't be able to vote for another three years." She recalled that she had an uncle who was a helicopter pilot during the Vietnam War. His helicopter was shot down and he was killed, prompting a discussion about widows.

"Uncle John and Aunt Teresa had a son who abandoned his wife and three preschool children," she whispered under her breath. Although the government provided some assistance, Taylor was told her aunt had raised her son's children but barely kept in touch with the rest of the family. Taylor thought it was odd that Helen didn't mention Philip's wife.

"I wonder what happened to them?" Taylor asked herself out loud.

"Maybe we should find out," Helen suggested. "Maybe you could check on your father's history, too," she added.

"Will you help me gramma?" the teen-ager pleaded.

"It's almost time for your mom to come to pick you up" said Helen. "Why don't we continue this next week and get going in the right direction?"

After Taylor's mom retrieved her daughter, Helen got on the telephone and asked a few relatives if they knew anything about Teresa Townsend; where she lived, what happened to her family and if she needed any help.

It took a few long days before Helen got the call she was waiting for: Bill, one of Teresa's grandsons--now in his twenties--explained why his grandmother didn't have a television or telephone in her home. "She hates commercials and robo calls, he said, and continued: "Why would anyone want to sell health insurance to an 85-year-old widow?"

"You're right," stammered Helen, "sometimes I feel like throwing something at my TV...anyhow, I'm glad you called. The first thing I want to talk about is your grandmother...how is my sister doing? When can we see her?"

"We are still in Northeast Ohio, where my grandparents and my grandparents' parents settled more than 120 years ago," he answered. "It's a little place in Trumbull County, one of the first counties carved out of the Western Reserve."

"Of course, you know that my granddad was killed in the Vietnam War," Bill, explained. "Then my dad left us."

"My grandmother had a hard time keeping us together... they wanted to put us in foster homes...she fought it in court... and she won!" he exclaimed. Right now, she spends a lot of time in bed, tended by nurses from a nearby health center and regular visits by me, my family, my two sisters and their families.

"Everything has been arranged for her funeral, including a Mass at St. James," he said...and ..so...if there's nothing else, I gotta go." and he abruptly hung up. Helen reluctantly called Taylor, her granddaughter, to tell her about Bill's call and the bad news about aunt Teresa. "It's no use," she said, "they just want to be left alone."

Helen thought it was kind of strange that Taylor didn't ask about her father.

The call aroused their curiosity about the fate of Bill's parents and the hundreds of war-widows from around the states after two world wars, Vietnam, Korea, Iran and Afghanistan, plus a dozen skirmishes on other foreign lands.

After a little research, they discovered how many widows were left behind when husbands sacrificed their lives in the War for Independence, the War of 1812, Indian wars, and the war between the states. About 25,000 soldiers were lost in the Revolutionary War--8,000 in battle and 17,000 from disease.

They decided to continue their search for the family's history by visiting the library and surfing the internet.

The library was within walking distance of her school. She stopped to talk with a few friends at the entrance, then saw a librarian. "My uncle's name was John Townsend," Taylor began. "He lived in Trumbull County. He was killed in Vietnam. I was hoping the library might have some kind of record showing his name and ancestry."

"We might have something," the librarian apologized, "but you could save much time and effort by consulting the Historic Society, the Veteran's Administration or go on-line with one of a dozen different genealogy outfits. Il'l give you a list of websites."

Taylor thanked the lady, disappointed but still determined to find out why her Aunt Teresa was avoiding any contact with the family.

In one of the books she borrowed, Taylor read that among the first immigrants to establish a settlement on American soil was a boatload of Pilgrims led by William Bradford in 1620 at Plymouth, Massachusetts. Their landing aboard the Mayflower, marked by the historic Plymouth Rock, was reportedly not fully recognized until many years after their arrival.

Taylor made a mental note to share more of the story about Plymouth with her grandmother.

"During the next twenty to thirty years there were boatloads after boatloads of Pilgrims and other religious denominations that found their way to the New England coastline," she recalled reading. 'Some headed for Plymouth--then one of the thirteen British colonies--and some that got only as far as Connecticut, another of the colonies."

In other books Taylor read were names of the settlers and their families--their ages, births, deaths and rank in the community. These had been carefully transcribed in town and church records--saved from destruction in Indian attacks that nearly wiped out settlement after settlement.

It was the Indian attacks, wild animals and the need to hunt for food, that forced most of the settlers to arm themselves, they said. The attacks motivated them to consider moving to a safer location. Protecting their families was a full-time job, she learned.

Taylor was eager to match the list of settlers with names

her grandmother might recognize...and sure enough...that was going to take some doing.

"Where do we start?" she asked her grandmother.

"Well, I guess, if you don't have very much background on your Aunt Teresa, we'll have to sign up with one of outfits that can help us find out what's troubling her," Helen answered. "Do you know her mother-in-law's maiden name?"

Helen asked a dozen more questions and all the answers were "no."

"Do we know where John Townsend was born?" she asked, again.

"Mom says the family has been living here in Trumbull County for over a hundred years, maybe more," Taylor replied.

"Maybe he's a descendant of one of the early settlers that came this way from the East Coast in the late 1700's."Helen suggested. "You never know."

"If he was, Taylor asked, "Wouldn't someone from around here have a record of it?"

"You have to remember honey, back in those days people kept records by hand, usually with a quill dipped in ink, in some kind of journal....they didn't have computers like you guys," remarked Helen "But maybe he was not a direct descendant," she added.

"What's the difference between a 'direct descendant' and any other kind of descendant?'" asked Taylor.

"Smart girl," choked Helen, "here's what I found: ... direct descendants, or lineal descendants, are the biological children and grandchildren of an ancestor. For example, you are a direct descendant of your mother, your grandmother, your great grandmother, and on and on. Collateral descendants are not part of the direct line; they are relatives descended from a sibling of an ancestor--such as uncles, aunts, nieces, nephews and cousins.

"Your aunt and cousin Bill are collateral descendants," Helen informed her young granddaughter. "Collateral and lineal descendants are both part of a family tree. Now, what else do we need to know?" she asked.

"Where do you get one of those family trees?" Taylor laughed.

"I can show you one," her aunt replied. From inside a folder stuffed with loose pages, Helen pulled out a drawing that listed the straight line direct decendantcy of a family's thirteen generations dating back to the mid-1600s. In the drawing--on a line drawn down the center of the page--is listed the name, date of birth, death and marriage of the first-born male of the previous generation. His children are listed beneath him in a horizontal line, with the oldest male in the center.

"Why only first-born males?" asked Taylor.

"You will have to ask the founding fathers," responded Helen. "They had a lot to do with setting up a new government after winning independence from the British...in those days," she added, "unless you were from a royal family, women--especially widows--were subject to the whims of male governors.

"It continues today," Helen aded. "Some countries require widows to wear black for the rest of their lives; some are required to marry a sibling from her husband's family. In some parts of Europe, including Russia, Czechoslovakia, Greece, Italy and Spain, widows used to wear black for the rest of their lives to signify their mourning, a practice that has since died out. In an article on Hinduism, said Helen, "a widow's head was shaved as part of her mourning; she could no longer wear a red dot on her forehead and was forbidden to wear jewels. She was also expected to walk barefoot."

"I'm glad we don't require anything like that here in America," chimed Taylor to her grandmother.

"In underdeveloped and developing areas of the world, conditions for widows continue to be much more severe," Helen responded. "There's a half-dozen countries that punish women for violating their regulations."

"Is that why so many men and women are eager to come to America?" Taylor asked her grandmother.

"It's hard to tell," she answered. "Each one has his or her reason, but mostly to seek freedom and an opportunity for a better life," she continued. "Take this for example," she added, unfolding the drawing of the family tree.

"An English minister, Helen pointed out," had all he could take from the royal family and decided to join a group sailing to America in the mid-1600s. He landed in Norwalk, a settlement in Connecticut, one of the thirteen British colonies established on the East Coast, and continued to make friends with some of the local Indians. One of the Indians, identified as Winnipank 'Sagmour of Norwalk' signed an agreement to give the minister a gift of a small island to "my beloved friend Thomas Hanford."

Helen continued: "The Rev. Hanford married a widow in 1661. They had eleven children, including Thomas I, his eldest son. One source says that Rev. Hanford probably died in 1693, leaving his widow, Mary, who died in 1730, 'aged one hundred years.' Most of the first eight generations included ten or more descendants. It was not unusual for men to produce large families by marrying a second or third time after the first wife died."

As they studied the family tree, Helen found an incident that threatened the family's line of direct decendantcy. It nearly ended with the ninth and tenth generation when Arthur George Hanford married Mary Demetri in 1905. They had one son, named Arthur Louis, who was only nine months old when he lost his father in a railroad accident. Arthur was still very young when his widowed Mother remarried and had four more children, all collateral descendants. When Arthur's oldest son, Arthur Jr., married, his male children all had girls.

It was important for the early settlers in Norwalk to have large families, Helen observed. "Women played an important role by securing a foothold for the future. It was hard work- -growing and hunting food, providing livable housing and

7

building communities. They felt uncomfortable being under a British governor and under constant surveillance by the English militia."

She also found that settlers had to contend with local Indian tribes who were upset by the increasing number of foreign settlements infringing on their hunting grounds; land that had been undisturbed for hundreds of years, long before Christopher Columbus paved the way to American soil in 1492.

It was a similar experience for Columbus, a deeply religious man, who bravely sought a trade route to Asia, Helen pointed out. Despite attempts to discredit Columbus for his achievements by including false information about his treatment of natives, most Americans favor continuing to observe Columbus Day on the second Monday of October, she said. The original date of the federal holiday, set by President Franklin D. Roosevelt and Congress in 1937, was October 12.

With the rapid growth in population in the mid-1700s, settlers sought a way to break away from royal domination by proposing an independent government. Leaders of the movement--later identified as the "Founding Fathers."--took it upon themselves to draft a Declaration of Independence. Among them were John Adams, Benjamin Franklin, Alexander Hamilton, John Jay and Thomas Jefferson.

John Adams and Thomas Jefferson, both later elected president of the United States, died on the same day--July 4, 1826. Each had six children. Jefferson married a widow--Martha Wayles--in 1772. George Washington, the first president, also married a widow--Martha Dandridge Custis. They had no children.

Among other early presidents that married widows were James Madison, who married Dolley Payne; and Andrew Jackson, who's wife, Rachel, died while aiding soldiers.

According to historians, Connecticut was originally settled by Dutch traders in 1633. They were said to be Puritans from the Massachusetts Bay Colony. After they arrived several more settlements were established in the colony, including Windsor, New Haven and Hartford.

Documents tell us life was difficult in those days. Men, women and children suffered from disease, extreme weather and wars with the indians. Much of the land settled by the colonists was bought from the Mohegan Indians. The Pequot tribe also wanted the land and, according to reports, "violence erupted" between the settlers and the Pequot Indians in 1637.

The settlement in Norwalk was not immune to the hardship caused by one Indian war after another, raids on its farms, violent deaths and the struggle for independence.

Connecticut, one of the smallest colonies shaped by the British, eventually was given permission to enlarge its territory with a strip of land running from the New England colonies to the West Coast. The permission to expand its territory was made possible by making some concessions with Pennsylvania and New York.

Its immediate effect, the history books tell us, was the formation of a group of investors who wanted to buy sections of the newly acquired land. Their quest for profit led to the designation of an area called the Western Reserve--a 120-mile-long strip of land bordering Lake Erie starting at the Pennsylvania state line.

"How is all this history going to help us find out what happened to my aunt and her family?" Taylor asked her grandmother, impatient and more curious than ever.

"Well, we have yet to find the Townsend name in any of the early colonial records," Helen admitted, "but we expect to have better luck after tracing families involved in the Revolutionary War and War of 1812. Then we can start tracing groups who made the long journey to the New Connecticut's Western Reserve."

The Revolutionary War, which began in 1775, lasted for almost eight years, Helen explained to her granddaughter. "Many of the colonists were killed during the War of 1812, when the British finally gave up and the new government began saving pension records of veterans and widows. Women were not well represented in early records, especially married women who often couldn't own land or vote," she added.

The widows were often left to fend for themselves as pioneers from the colonies explored routes to the New Connecticut in Ohio and and began settlements along the way. Ohio, which became a state in 1801, was only sparsely populated when immigrants began pouring in.

Streams of settlers had been dragging wagons across the uncharted mountain passes to get to the once-popular Salt Spring Region as early as 1755. The salt, produced from the brackish water in ponds area near the Pennsylvania border and other locations, was very scarce but necessary for the preservation of meat in an era before refrigeration.

Colonists knew that Indians claimed ownership of the territory where the springs were located. Their presence made them reluctant to buy the land upon which salt springs sat, and thus antagonize the Indians. People who had hope of making fortunes from the mineral water rode horseback for long treks back and forth to their homesteads. They spent long hours boiling the water in buckets to get the salt but eventually gave up and abandoned the idea.   This condition changed after the Revolutionary War and Connecticut became part of the United States. Connecticut had to give up its claim to this area. The western part of the Reserve was given by the state of Connecticut to people whose farms and homes were burned out by the British during the Revolutionary War. That part of the Western Reserve became known as the 'Fire Lands.'

Before the Revolutionary War, a group of land speculators in Connecticut formed *The Connecticut Land Company* and bought the remainder of the Reserve for about 43 cents an acre. At this time, historians observed, the Reserve was then opened for settlement to all who possessed the daring and fortitude to make the journey to the wilderness area.

A commission, composed of Yale graduates, was empowered by the Connecticut Land Company to conduct a survey of the Reserve, layout townships, establish rules, sell land and make concessions with Indians and neighboring states. Yale was founded in 1701 in New Haven, Connecticut. Western Reserve College, instituted in 1826, was referred to as the Yale of the West.

The commission named investors and a board of directors, which quickly divided up the 3,400,000-acre Western Reserve into townships of 16,000 acres each. Among the investors was Henry Champion, a war veteran married to Abigail Tinker and father of eight children. Champion and fellow investor Moses Clevealand were appointed to a board of directors that hired surveyors and a crew of about fifty, including two women, to make the journey and map out the new Connecticut Western Reserve.

In the original records of the survey excursion, there's a full list of employees given with these words "and two females." It was not unusual for a bookkeeper to omit a woman's name "unless she were a queen or a sorcerer," the record said. For those that are interested, the "two women" were Ann, the wife of Elija Gun and Tabitha Currie, the wife of Job Stiles.

When the survey team, headed by Moses Clevealand, finally arrived on the shores of Lake Erie, they were overjoyed by the landscape and eager to celebrate the twentieth anniversary of the nation's independence on July 4.

As the surveyors were mapping the Reserve, the British continued to challenge the United States' claim of independence and set out to block any further expansion to the West. The War of 1812 put a nail in the English plan to take over any part of American soil, but at a huge cost in men's lives and their plans to settle in a new land.

"We are fortunate that the most revealing records for female ancestors are found in military pensions," said Helen, noting that she had a list of three valuable indexes for the

War of 1812 that can be reached online. The list, which she handed to her granddaughter, suggested contact with the National Archives and Veterans Administration for: "Case files of pension applications;" the "Old War Pension Index" and "Index to pension application files of remarried widows."

"If your uncle or any of his ancestors are listed in those records, it might give us a lead to why your aunt and cousin are avoiding the family," Taylor's grandmother concluded.

"Call me if you find anything before we get together again next week. It could be interesting."

CHAPTER II

THE INTOLERABLE ACTS

While still at the library, Helen was determined to find some clues about the Townsend family among the first settlers of the Western Reserve.

Helen browsed through several volumes describing the adventures of men who kept journals on their early visit to the Reserve after long journeys from Eastern Connecticut.

Among the books was a narrative by Henry Leavitt Ellsworth, son of Oliver Ellsworth, who bought forty-one thousand acres of Reserve property from the Connecticut Land Company. Oliver, who played a significant role in the formation of the country, had proposed the name "United States" for the new nation.

Helen reminisced with her granddaughter about Abigail Wolcott. "You might find this interesting," she said.

Oliver married Abigail Wolcott in 1772. She became a widow in 1807 and reportedly remained active in civic affairs, including public support for a Bicarmel Congress with two houses--the House of Representatives and U.S. Senate-- adopted at the Constitutional Convention in 1787

Helen and Taylor shuffled from one bookshelf to another looking for incidents in American History that might help them in their search for Taylor's aunt and uncle. When each located a book that seemed promising, they grabbed a table near a library window to share what they found.

Helen, her hands trembling as she leafed through a thick history book, explained to Taylor why she chose to read about the American Revolution. In 1774, the British Parliament passed a series of laws the Americans described as the "Intolerable Acts," she read.

"What in the world were so intolerable," asked Taylor.

Helen gave her a brief explanation: "The laws were designed, according to members of Congress, to punish colonists for defying British policies," she said. "The 'Acts,' which closed the Boston port, forbade town meetings and required colonists to house British soldiers on demand, among other "unjust and cruel" acts, prompted an effort to declare the colonies independent from British rule.

The British response to the declaration was an engagement with colonists at Lexington, Massachusetts, where a contingent of British soldiers attacked patriots assembled to train for possible hostilities. The attack, on April 19, 1775, was the first military engagement of the American Revolutionary War. Eight soldiers were killed, including Ensign Robert Monroe.

"Everybody knows about Paul Revere," Taylor reminded her grandmother. "Revere was the one who alerted the colonists that the British army was coming by signaling from the Old North Church in Boston."

"Don't forget Marquis de Lafayette," said Helen, "a French citizen who was appointed a major general in the Continental Army; and Ethan Allen, who is best known for assisting in the capture of Fort Ticonderoga in upstate New York."

The Declaration of Independence was adopted at a meeting of the Second Continental Congress in Philadelphia on July 4, 1776. John Adams persuaded a committee to select Thomas Jefferson to compose the original draft of the document. It announced that the thirteen American colonies, then at war with the Kingdom of Great Britain, regarded themselves as thirteen independent sovereign states no longer under British rule. These states would found a new nation – the United States of America.

A few years after Oliver died, Abigail and her six surviving children decided it was time to check out progress on the sale of their huge tract of land. Her son Henry wrote the narration published in a book about his 10-week tour of the sparsely populated Reserve.

"We can talk about Henry's tour later," Helen begged her granddaughter. "Right now I'd like to go to my place where I can tell you about some of the other things I found.

"It is no secret that many of America's founders were raised by widows who inspired them," Helen said, then added "Henry later served as mayor of Hartford and other positions, including The father of the United States Department of Agriculture. His twin brother William gained distinction as governor of Connecticut."

The books Helen read eventually provided information about men from the Hanford family that served in American wars. They left a long list of widows she hoped would help identify her granddaughter's ancestry. Among Hanford men who served in the Revolutionary War between 1775 and 1783 was Abraham, who had married Anna Selleck and settled in Oneida County, New York, with nine children.

Other Hanford men that served as veterans of the Revolution, she went on, were Austin, son of Theophilus, a direct descendant of the Rev. Thomas Hanford, and three of his brothers--Ebenezer, Theophilus and Timothy. Austin, who died in the War of 1812, was married to Betty Sterling. They had four children.

Also listed among Hanford's who served in the Revolution were: Ebenezer, one of only three men who were awarded the Badge of Military Merit by then General George Washington. Daniel, who was taken prisoner by the British and held in the infamous Sugar House Prison in New York; Hezekiah, who enlisted at age 58; Jeremiah; one of seven Hanford brothers from Rome, NY; Jesse, a resident of Norwalk; John, who served in the 9th Connecticut Regiment, and Noah, who was listed as a drummer in the Connecticut Militia.

Also identified as veterans of the revolution, Helen continued, were Obidiah; Levi; Matthew; Phineas; Theophilus III; Timothy; Stephen; and James Richards. A cemetery in Norwalk contains many Hanford graves and the graves of more than 40 early settlers.

According to military records, Phineas served as a corporal in the 9th Regiment Militia under Captain Ozias Marvin, which at the time was the Coast Guard. The 9th Regiment was present at the "Burning of Norwalk" raid by British troops led by General Tyron on July 10, 1779.

Helen continued to discuss events of the that period, unsure if she had her granddaughter on the right track.

The British set ablaze 130 homes, 40 shops, ten barns, five ships, and two churches. Only six homes were spared, all belonging to Loyalists. 800 militia and Continental Army troops fought more than 2,600 British and Hessian troops. General Tyron took many prisoners back to New York where more than 60% died on British prison ships.

"Ooh--my God...I can understand why they were so angry!" Taylor blurted, as her grandmother continued to relate what she had learned at the library.

She also told about the numerous widows with young families that were able to take advantage of an offer of free property in the western part of the state called the "Fire Lands". That part of the state--about 500,000 acres--was given to people whose farms and homes were burned out by the British during the Revolutionary War.

The Connecticut Land Company, which had established regulations for development of the entire territory and divided the New Connecticut Western Reserve into townships of 16,000 acres each, set boundaries for thirteen counties--Ashtabula,

Geauga, Cuyahoga, Lake, Trumbull, Mahoning, Portage, Summit and parts of Medina, Ashland, Erie, Huron and Lorain.

The company also helped settlers locate potential homesteads by dividing the land into lots five miles square, and identifying the lots in a map by range and town number. The "townships" were numbered from the base line northward to Lake Erie, and the "ranges" westward from the Pennsylvania border. Cleaveland, named after Moses Cleaveland, who led the survey, was designated as No. 7 in the twelfth range.

The rules and regulations of the Connecticut Land Company provided for the possibility of misunderstanding, noted Helen. Minor details are mentioned. Historians said It had the workmanship of the careful, conservative New England mind. The directors of the company were Oliver Phelps, Henry Champion, Roger Newberry, and Samuel Mathews, Jr. They reportedly had no trouble adding conditions to the sale of their newly acquired land. The first townships had to provide a grist mill and sawmill. If a salt spring was found in a township, settlers had to reserve the spring together with 2,000 acres of enclosing land.

The grist mills and saw mills were important to settlements. Without a grist mill, the women had to grind wheat and other grains by hand to make flour for making bread, a staple in the their diet. Some of the mills were elaborate--some powered by a water wheel, wind or livestock. A sawmill employed the use of a circular blade powered by water to cut trees into lumber.

Most cabins, usually built near the center of their parcel of land, were constructed by settlers using logs cut by hand from trees. The logs were laid horizontally and interlocked on the ends with notches. Depending on where and how well they were built, a settler and his family could construct a basic log cabin within a few days, one historian said.

The townships, once they were established, kept records of their inhabitants for no better reason other than paying taxes. Widows, it seems, were of little concern until the new

17

government came up with a plan to provide benefits for a husband's service. Even then, a widow (or her heirs) had to prove that her husband died of wounds suffered in a war before benefits became available.

As years went by, the number pension applications received at the Veteran's Association increased. They were digitized, giving descendants an opportunity to piece together the lives of those mystery women in their families. Which was exactly what Helen and her granddaughter where preparing to do... when they heard someone knocking on her front door.

It was Bill Townsend...disheveled...a big guy with a few extra pounds. He stood there for a few moments waving a large enveloper. He took a deep breath and shouted: "What in the hell or you doing? I told you to leave us alone!"

Frightened, Taylor and her grandmother, tried to calm him down. "Come on in," she begged Bill, as he stood in the doorway, shaking like a leaf.

"Can I get you something?" she asked. "Soda, water... coffee?

"You got a beer," he replied...and Helen rushed to the kitchen refrigerator where she had a couple of bottles set aside for situations like this.

"Now...what's this all about?" she asked, as he took a long swig on the bottle.

"You know damn well what this is about, nosing into our family's history and sending someone from the Veteran's Association to file an application for benefits," he said sarcastically. "Why don't you check out your own family history while you are at it!"

"We had no intention of violating your privacy," Helen pleaded, "we are looking for family ancestors that may have settled in the Western Reserve about 200 years ago. We thought it would be good to know where they came from, how they lived, if they served in the military and if we have any other relatives from around here that we don't know about."

After a few moments, Taylor, sauntered into the living room to join the conversation. "I have never met Aunt Teresa," she politely said to Bill as he took another swig on the beer. "Is there any reason why we can't see her?"

"I told you she wants to be left alone...and that is all I can tell you," he responded. "If she changes her mind, I will let you know...otherwise please keep us out of your search." With that, Bill rose from his chair and headed for the door.

"You will let us know if there is anything we can do for Teresa..won't you?" leaded Helen.

He stared at her for a moment, mumbled a few words, slammed the door...and left.

The eerie silence that followed was broken when Taylor cried out "Oh gramma!"

They hugged for a while...then talked about what they were going to do next.

"What did he mean about checking your family?" Taylor asked.

"My family name is not important," she said,"Teresa and I are sisters that married when we were very young .... but if you must know my father's name was Henry Beck."

They had several internet addresses for outfits willing to provide users with information about possible ancestors... but at a price, if you care to join. They decided to go back to the library and conduct a free search through church history books.

In articles about the first colonists from Connecticut to settle in the Western Reserve they found church records for the United Presbyterian Church from Farmington, in Trumbull County; the Brecksville Congregational Church in Cuyahoga County; the First Congregational Church from Randolph in Portage County; the Fist Congregational Church in Kent, from the Portage County; the Mount Leigh Presbyterian Church from Adams County; and Regular Baptist Church records in Geauga County.

There was no mention of the Townsend or Beck name in early Trumbull County church records.

They did, however, find a reference to a Rev. William Hanford in the files of the old Cleveland Leader. According go the article, William--a collateral descendant of Rev. Thomas Hanford-- and the Rev. Randolph Stone organized the First Presbyterian Church that later became the Old Stone Church, a landmark on Cleveland's Public Square. The two ministers organized the church in 1820 with 18 members in the congregation, none of them named Townsend. The church was rebuilt several times after destructive fires.

They examined records of other churches in the city, including the historic Cathedral of St. John the Evangelist, established in the 1840s. The church is the cathedral of the Roman Catholic Diocese of Cleveland. No Townsends there, either...they learned.

"We need to go back and review names of the early settlers," said Helen, "maybe we missed women who became widows after husbands died from injuries suffered in the War for Independence."

"That's a good idea," thought Taylor,"

"There was no shortage of heroes during the American Revolution," noted Helen," including many brave women who risked their lives to win independence for the American colonies." She then went on to read from a list of famous people lost to history. "These," she said, "are a few that have not been forgotten."

Abigail Adams, the wife of John Adams, who helped him with many important decisions during the war. She helped provide the Continental Army with food and shelter.

Mary Draper, who helped the soldiers of the Continental Army by providing them with food, clothing and ammunition. It is said, she melted her own pewter platters and mugs to make bullets for the soldiers.

Mary Catherine Moore helped General Morgan defeat

British General Cornwallis at the Battle of Cowpens, a key battle towards the end of the war.

The lack of recognition among women became apparent in 1895 when a committee organized to celebrate Cleveland's role in the growth of the Western Reserve gave a report with little or no mention of wives "...who," the report said, "had performed an equal though different part in laying the foundation of future civilization and prosperity."

As an example, among the pioneer women listed in the report who settled in Middlefield, Ohio, were: Polly Thompson, wife of Stephen Bond; Betsy Young, wife of Isaac Gates; Isabella Porter, wife of James McElroy; Lydia Thompson, wife of Moses Morse; Mary Rice, wife of Sam Russell; Jane Johnson, second wife of Capt. Isaac Thompson; Mercy Tracy, second wife of James Thompson; Lucinda Walden, wife of William Thompson; Rebecca Menaugh, wife of Robert Wallace; Rachel Dailey, wife of Benjamin White; Lydia Everts, wife of Lathrop Wilson; and Hannah Carroll, wife of Silas Young.

A large number of the men who settled in Middlefield and other townships in the Reserve were listed as soldiers in the Ohio Militia during the War for Independence.

The exact number of deaths In the war is unknown but it has been reported that Smallpox took more lives than any battle. The estimated amount of deaths due to Smallpox was 130,000 people. There were an estimated 25,000 American soldiers who died...8,000 of them came from battle-connected deaths and the other 17,000 deaths came from disease. Thousands of British and German soldiers also died in battle or from disease, the report said.

Taylor was eager to find any mention of the Townsend family, but it was getting late and her mother would be expecting her. As they drove up the short driveway, they could see her standing on the porch--arms folded across her chest and a sour look on her face.

"What's wrong mom," she asked, "are you okay?"

"Taylor!!" she cried, "where have you been?"

"With gramma...at the library.

"Tell your gramma good-bye...and come in here,"she asked.

Bewildered, but obedient, Taylor searched for something to say to her grandmother, as tears ran down her face. "I'll call you," she sputtered. "Don't worry...I will be okay."

With that, she turned on her heels, climbed the porch steps and followed her mom into the house. She could hear Helen backing out of the driveway.

There were some uneasy moments as Taylor waited for her mother to explain what was bothering her.

"I got some disturbing phone calls about this thing you and your grandmother are doing," she huffed. "You are making me nervous and some people very unhappy...I don't want you to be seeing your grandmother anymore!"

"You are old enough to take care of yourself" she added, "you don't need a babysitter anymore."

"But mom," Taylor pleaded, "I enjoy being with gramma. I've learned a lot more about our country than we got in school and she's helping me study how women, especially widows, enabled settlement of the Western Reserve. What's so wrong with that?"

"There are some relatives that may have a reason for wanting to be left alone..." snipped her mother. Her response cut short.

"You have been talking with my cousin Bill Townsend," interrupted Taylor. "I think he is trying to hide something about his past...wouldn't you like to know what it is?"

"Not particularly," she replied, "I've got better things to do."

The squabbling simmered down as they prepared dinner that evening, Taylor offered to wash the dishes and got her mother to lift the ban on talking to her grandmother. She called her and went to bed.

Over the weekend, they continued their search for relatives among victims of the war for independence. Among their sources were books by Harriet Taylor Upton (no relation to Helen's granddaughter) and Getrude Van Rensselaer. Upton, a widow, wrote "The Pioneers of New Connecticut," a dissertation on the history of the Western Reserve, and Van Rensselaer, also a widow, wrote about pioneer women and families in the Western Reserve.

Rensselaer, widow of Capt. Samuel Wickham, who died in 1869, wrote how widows from the thirteen colonies contributed to the fight for independence. With the termination of British control over Western Connecticut, settlers began pouring into the area.

The names of wives and widows become much more evident in records kept after the War of 1812, she said. Many Hanford's emigrated to the state of New York from Norwalk and New Canaan, Connecticut, settling in more than 36 different towns and villages throughout the state between 1800 and 1900.

Among victims of the War of 1812 was Elizabeth Tyler, widow of Private George Tyler of the Maryland militia. He was a seaman on one of the ships that participated in the battle of Fort McHenry, which inspired Frances Scott Key to write The Star Spangled Banner.

"Not to change the subject, but there still is some controversy over who designed the American flag," noted Helen. "Although historians recount a visit to Philadelphia by George Washington and a committee to meet with Betsy Ross to discuss the flag, it may have been one of several flag makers who came up with the original idea. Ross was the widow of Col. George Ross, a delegate from Pennsylvania to Congress."

"It didn't make any difference who designed it," said Helen, "the patriots were always proud to carry the stars and stripes into battle."

After the war for independence was finally over and a Constitution was in place, the colonists got around to developing townships in various parts of the Reserve.

Moses Clevealand, who led a detachment of surveyors to map out the Western Reserve, was so impressed with the landscape at the mouth of the Cuyahoga River that he selected it as a spot for a city. After "exasperating" trade with Indians, his staff named it Clevealand--a name changed to Cleveland, without the "a" to make it fit in a headline.

The city grew quickly. According to one account, It had the first grist mill in the state; the first dry goods store; the first missionary; the first distillery; the first school and the first postmaster. It also held the first funeral and the first wedding, among other firsts.

Other cities and towns in the Reserve area that grew quickly, and with less bloodshed, were Hudson, founded in 1799; Youngstown, founded in 1796; Warren in 1798; Ravenna in 1799; Ashtabula in 1803, and Stow in 1804.   Hudson   is where the Western Reserve College was founded in 1826.

In 1801, Warren was established as the seat of Trumbull County, which then encompassed the entire Connecticut Western Reserve. This distinction was said to enhance Warren's status as the religious, social, and commercial hub of the early Western Reserve. Warren referred to itself as the capital of the Western Reserve.

Before the city could capitalize on its success, the new nation had to survive another attempt by the British to take over the territory.

CHAPTER III

WAR SLOWS EXPANSION

Helen and her granddaughter enjoyed sitting on Helen's porch for their weekly sessions on family history. On the agenda, depending on the weather, was what they had discovered since their meeting last week.

They began by sharing stories about settlers helping widows and survivors of the revolution make the long journey from the East Coast to establish homesteads in the Reserve.

"Just talking about those long trips is making me thirsty," said Helen, who made some lemonade, poured herself a glass and invited her granddaughter to do the same.

"What did you find?" asked Taylor, as she took a sip and slowly opened a notebook computer to impress her grandmother. It contained articles about the massive movement of early pioneers eager to buy land from investors... sight unseen.

Among those that made the trip, Helen recalled, was Rev. William Hanford, a relative of Rev. Thomas Hanford.

'What else did I find?" she asked as she sorted reports from a stack of notes, The Connecticut Western Reserve of Ohio was still mostly wilderness with only a few small towns and villages scattered across the landscape, she began. Ohio just became a state within the last decade. Indian tribes living in the area were forced to give up their land and move west.

Most roads were former Indian trails, with horseback, buggies, stagecoaches and wagons the only means of overland transportation. Very little law enforcement had been established. It was frontier land waiting to be developed, she explained.

A church was the central place where people could gather and form a bond. In the early 1800s, the Church was as much a form of local government as it was a religious organization. Most services were held in log cabins or in a barn with only a handful of worshipers. Regardless of the setting, it gave the pioneers a sense of security and a reason to create new roots.

"This is how settler communities were born," Helen advised her granddaughter, who was doing her best to draw attention.

Helen told her about the Reverend William Hanford, who played a significant role in the formation of as many as twenty pioneer churches in Ohio. His travels, which began in the early 1800s' at the age of 26, took him to every known settlement in the entire Connecticut Western Reserve, including Cleveland. He was also a staunch abolitionist and used his home as part of the Underground Railroad in helping black slaves escape to Canada.

Rev.William Hanford was the first resident minister of the Congregational Church in Twinsburg and the first Secretary of the Board of Trustees of Western Reserve College in Hudson.

Hudson had an historic role in the fight against slavery. It was a famous stop on the Underground Railroad and home to celebrated abolitionist John Brown. Hudson bore witness to many of the sentiments that caused the Civil War and divided a nation, Helen pointed out.

Among other American religious leaders that toured Ohio then was Joseph Smith, founder of Mormonism. By 1900, other prominent denominations in Ohio were Roman Catholic,

Methodist, and Presbyterian. There were also groups of Baptists, Lutherans, and Society of Friends.

The War of 1812, which began on June 18, 1812, was a conflict between the United States and the United Kingdom, Helen continued. It began as naval blockades to choke off contested trade and blossomed into raids on American settlers expanding to the West.

The Royal Navy's blockade of the American Coast infuriated the American Congress, so they declared war. A few members of Congress reportedly saw the war as an opportunity to annex Canada.

In battles at sea and across North America, thousands of British and American soldiers and sailors were killed, injured or taken as prisoners, leaving widows on both sides of the Atlantic. The heaviest fighting was said to have taken place in campaigns at St. Lawrence; Baltimore; Detroit; Pittsburg; Chesapeake; New Orleans; the Battle of Lake Erie and the Battle of the Thames.

On August 24, 1814, the British set fire to the Capitol and the White House in the nation's capital. President James Madison and First Lady Dolly Madison were forced to flee the city, but not before Dolly arranged to save some famous paintings, including a rare portrait of President George Washington.

After more than two years of war and casualties on both sides, the two countries signed the Treaty of Ghent, which ended the war with no border changes. The treaty was unanimously ratified on February 17, 1815.

"What effect did that war have on settlements in the Western Reserve?" inquired Taylor, who was narrowing her search for anything about her uncle's family.

"I'm getting to that," said Helen, who had been online with the Veteran's Administration studying case files of pension applications based on death or disability incurred by servicemen during the War of 1812. The basic files, she was told, are for all soldiers and/or their widows. Not all applicants were approved, she noted, but the names were still on record at the National Archives in Washington, DC.

"It was a very difficult time for women" she explained. "If a widow remarried, the payments would stop. If she became a widow again, she could reapply to have the pension payments renewed. She told Taylor that the Federation of Genealogical Societies was in the midst of photographing and digitizing all the soldiers' pensions from the War of 1812.

"As more pensions are digitized, there are more opportunities to piece together the lives of those mystery women in our families," she concluded.

The comment gave Taylor an opening for her presentation. As she drew herself closer to the shiny glass-top table in front of her, she began to let her grandmother know just how smart she was.

"The Western Reserve Historical Society in Cleveland has one of the nation's largest collection of journals kept by colonists as they traveled from Connecticut to the Western Reserve between 1796 and 1822...lots of good stuff here," she said.

"My cousin Bill told us his grandfather's grandfather had settled in Trumbull County more than 120 years ago," she recalled, "there has to be some kind of record there," she said, adding, "I have a sneaky feeling that my great aunt is in danger."

"What makes you think that?" her grandmother quickly replied...concerned about the implication.

"Well, let's say somebody in your brother-in-laws family was caught illegally collecting pension benefits when his widow lied about the date of their wedding. Let's say your sister knows who it is and has been keeping her secret for more than fifty years.

"You're dreaming!" mocked Helen. "We have nothing to indicate that she's in any kind of trouble...especially if it has anything to do with military benefits...the less you say about that the better."

"That's part of the trouble," Taylor responded, "people who kept records during the early days of the Reserve, the Revolution and other wars didn't bother to include the names of women."

One thing they noticed, however, was the prominence given to biographies of men, living or dead, who had been identified with the settlement and growth of the Reserve, with little or no mention of their wives ... wives who had performed an equal, though different, part in laying the foundations of future civilization.

Missing from public records--except at the Western Reserve Library-- are stories that include the names of pioneer married couples, their locations, dates, their entire list of children with children's marriage partners.

Among the women acknowledged in stories about the growth of the Western Reserve was Ascenath Biddlecomb, who married Alonzo Hosmer in 1822. The couple became the parents of ten children.

Also mentioned, added Taylor, were:

Mary Marsden, who eloped from a comfortable home near Pittsburgh with John McLaughlin, a Roman Catholic. Because of his faith her father disinherited her. Later, they sought a home on the Reserve in 1806, and she swam her horse across the Mahoning River with a child in her arms, afterwards known as Aunt Jane McKinnie.

Mr. and Mrs. Crispin Mennel, nee Elizabeth Melburn, formerly from Yorkshire, England, who came to Grafton in 1826. They bought a farm on which they resided during their lives. She kept a dairy many years, and excelled in cheese and butter making.

Other English women who came about the same time from Yorkshire were: Mrs. William Richardson, Mary Dalton, Mrs. John Coleman, Sarah Strattler, Mrs. John Langdale,

Hepsibah Clark, Mrs. Moses Dafter (Ellen Alexander), Mrs. Joseph Johnson (Ann Brown), Mrs. William Rosindale (Jane Brown), Mrs. Samuel Alexander (Sarah Francom), Mrs. Robert Wilson (Mary Toney), Mrs. Thomas Scrage (Elizabeth Burdette), Mrs. Joseph Salsbury (Mary Grasby), Mrs Robert Blantern (Elizabeth Turner), Mrs. Urias (Elizabeth Spence) Noble.

"All these were remarkably tidy and thrifty homemakers, noted one historian. "They walked erect and wore white caps which gave them a very neat appearance in any costume."

Months prior to the end of the Revolutionary War, the British invaded Connecticut and destroyed by fire the towns of New London, Greenville, Fairfield, Danbury, Ridgefield, Norwalk, New Haven," East Haven and Groton. Benedict Arnold, then a British general, personally oversaw the destruction of New London. More than 1800 supporters of the American Revolution suffered in the devastation of those nine towns.

The carnage put a damper on expansion of the new nation, but brought a stream of immigrants to Ohio, Taylor explained.

Early settlement in Cleveland and the Western Reserve is documented extensively through the personal papers of early settlers, survey maps, newspapers, and the records of early businesses. These early settlers were followed by waves of immigration that included German farmers, Irish workers, and Jewish communities.

Early settlements were made in Conneaut, Ashtabula County, in 1796; Cleveland, Cuyahoga County, in 1796; Youngstown, Mahoning County,in 1796; Harpersfield, Ashtabula County, in 1798; Warren, Trumbull County, in 1798; Burton, Geauga County, in 1798; Austinburg, Ashtabula County, in 1799; and Ashtabula in Ashtabula County in 1799.

An agreement with Indians to prevent settlement of white men on land northwest of the Ohio River, was temporarily enforced by the U.S.Army. Soldiers were ordered to burn their huts and eliminate stragglers.

"That was not an easy thing to witness," said one of the

widows who later managed to escape through barriers set up on the west end of the Western Reserve.

"Relax honey," interjected Helen, Taylor's grandmother, who was anxious to report on hardships women experienced in those days.

"I have some background on the development of settlements in Trumbull County," she explained. Browsing through a version of the history of the Western Reserve by Harriett Taylor Upton, Helen explained how the settlement began.

"James Kingsbury may be considered the first permanent settler in old Trumbull County," Helen reported, "Stiles and Gun were ahead of him with the party, but Gun only stayed a little while, three or four years," she learned.

She was also told of evidence that proved Kingsbury to be a valued citizen. The following was found among papers of Judge Turhand Kirtland:

"May 18, 1811. Rec'd, Cleveland, of Turhand Kirtland a deed from the trustees of the Connecticut Land Company for 100 acres, lot No. 433, being the same lot that was voted by said company to be given to said Kingsbury and wife for a compensation for early settlement, and sundry services rendered said company with me." Signed: "James Kingsbury."

After the Connecticut Land Company had withdrawn its surveyors, the emigrants who appeared settled in isolated spots. This was because they bought land in large amounts and because the Connecticut Land Company scattered them so much.

Settlers were thus lonesome, far away from base supplies, and obliged to grind their own corn and grain, found trouble in procuring domestic animals, in having implements repaired, or in securing the services of a physician.

Among the early troubles of the housewife was getting of the material for the bread making. Mills were far distant; at first in Pennsylvania, then Youngstown, Warren and Cleveland.

Many families utilized a hollowed stump with a long pole from which a stone was suspended for grinding corn and grain.

The hand mills which came later required two hours' grinding to supply one person with food for one day. Sometimes wheat would get wet, or was not properly harvested, and bread would run despite the greatest efforts of the homemaker.

Baking powder was unknown, and sour milk and saleratus was used for lightbreads; the latter was made by the homemaker herself from ashes. The bread was known as "salt-rising" or "milk-rising," and required no hop yeast.

If this fermented too long it would spoil, and the empties would have to be made again. As cows became more numerous, the churning and cheese-making grew heavier. There was no ice in summer, and churning would sometimes occupy half a day.

Cheese was made in huge tubs or hollowed logs on the floor, and we wonder how women ever could stoop over and stir curd by the hour, as they were obliged to do.

They dried the wild berries, and later the apples, peaches, and other fruits; they rendered their land, dried and corned their beef, put in pickle their pork, and when winter closed down, after 1800, almost every cabin had provisions enough to keep the family from want, and most of this had been prepared by the homemaker.

Investors expected that the northern part of the Western Reserve would be settled before the southern, but the opposite was true.

The bits of land cleared long before, lying in the lower part, seemed very inviting to those who had attempted to remove the huge trees covering almost the entire section.

Among the first settlers were men who walked the entire way from Connecticut; some rode horseback part way, sharing the horse with others; some rode in ox carts; some drove oxen; some came part way by land and the rest by water; some came on sleds in midwinter; some plowed through the mud of spring, or endured the heat of summer; some had bleeding feet, and some serious illnesses.

Sometimes it was bride and a groom who started alone; sometimes it was a husband, wife and children; sometimes it was a group of neighbors who made the party. Children were born on the way, and people of all ages died and were buried where they died.

Among other early settlers in Trumbull County, the story goes, was John Young, who emigrated from New York and in 1792 married Mary Stone White. He began his settlement, calling it Youngstown, in lower Trumbull in 1796. They had two children.

James Hillman, a friend of Young who was in the business of transporting passengers and trading with Indians and frontiersmen, helped Young lay out the town. The next year James Kingsbury and his family were there, together with Major Lorenzo Carter and Ezekiel Holley and their families. In 1798, Rodolphus Edwards and Nathaniel Doan and family were added to the colony.

One of the stories that emerged out of that period was the reference to one of the settlers as "The Daniel Boone of Trumbull County." He was one of three brothers--Delaun, Asehel and Isaac Mills-- that made the trip to the Western Reserve in a covered wagon. The trip was more expensive than they expected and they had less than twenty-five cents when they arrived. They went to work for one of the surveyors and settled in different parts of the Reserve. Delaun Mills, who had a reputation as a great hunter of both animals and Indians, entertained early travelers with his adventures as the "Daniel Boone of Trumbull County."

Without a physician and in possession of only a few medicines, settlers used whatever nature could provide. For calomel, they substituted pills from the extract of bark of the butternut, and in lieu of quinine, used dog-wood and cherry bark. Probably because of this malarious condition, and

33

because of the severe winds, the colony at the mouth of the Cuyahoga did not grow, and from January, 1799, to April,1800, Major Carter's family was the only one living there," the report said.

"If they were having such a hard time why did they continue to make the journey?" interrupted Taylor, who was searching for ancestors among early settlers in the Western Reserve.

"You have to remember," Helen pointed out, "many of the early settlers who bought land in the highly touted New Connecticut, were expecting to find a paradise to plant roots for their families. They had disposed of property back East and packed up all their belongings before making the trip. There was no place else for them to go."

Under the hardships and exposures, with the long hours of work and the large families, women died early. Most men had two wives in their lifetime.

Occasionally a father and mother would both die and leave the children to care for themselves. Several cases are given in early records and letters of girls who reared their little brothers and sisters in their primitive cabins.

One such girl, eleven years old, kept house for three younger children and was herself married at sixteen to a boy aged nineteen. The community watched over these young folks and called them "babes in the woods."

They themselves were the parents of six girls and seven boys. Families were large in those days, but, although people had many children, the percent which grew to mature years is so small as to be startling.

When churches began to be built, women contributed in work, not only in furnishing but even in raising the building. One woman solicited small donations of wool from people of the vicinage and wove a carpet for the church.

Many of the women were devoted Christians and traveled many miles on Sunday by horseback, sometimes taking two children with them, to attend services. These women allowed little or no work to be done on Sunday. Cows, of course, must be milked, and stock fed, but no cooking was permitted. Beds were aired all day and made up after sundown.

"Although people did their duty," explained Helen, "there was more sorrow then than now, more discomfort then than now, less freedom then than now. There was less open expression of love, and more repressed feeling of all kind."

Women were tired and worn out, and, in many cases, scolded. Men were sometimes overbearing, sometimes drunken, and occasionally cruel, she added.

A pleasant woman living in the early days of old Trumbull county, when quite young, lost her husband. She continued to reside for a little time in her lonesome cabin, but later was induced to marry a man of the neighborhood who had several children.

After a time he became abusive and she was afraid he would take her life. Because of superstition, he was afraid to go into the graveyard after dusk. The only place, therefore, that she was absolutely safe was in the cemetery, and many a night she slept in peace on her first husband's grave.

CHAPTER IV

GROWING PAINS

"Well," said Helen, as she took in a deep breath, "why can't we find something about your Uncle John or your Aunt Teresa?"

Taylor was concerned. "Other than the 23,000 times the name comes up in an online search, there doesn't seem to be much hope...is there gramma?"

"Its too early to give up...we just haven't looked in the right places," Helen said as she embraced her granddaughter. "Let's take a break. I'll take you home and we'll get back to our search next Friday."

As they approached Taylor's home, Helen could see Taylor's mother standing on the porch, waiting for her daughter to come home. She thought about what the woman, a widow like her, could be doing at this time of the day.

She was pleasantly surprised to see Cynthia wearing an apron standing at the door. "Come on in," she beckoned, as she toweled off her hands.

"Somebody's birthday...and I'm baking a cake," she explained, with a big toothy smile.

At first, there was some awkward silence...then "Mom, you don't bake!" chided her daughter. They laughed for a moment...then sat down next to a flour-covered table strewn with flour-covered bowls, cups, and baking utensils.

"What do you mean...I don't bake...don't be silly...I can read a recipe...and I don't have to grind the flour myself!" Cynthia joked. She quickly acknowledged that she has been reading some of Taylor's notes about the problems experienced by early settlers of the Western Reserve.

"But mom," Taylor implored, "why a cake?" "Whose birthday?" she asked.

"Its your fathers," she responded. "He would have been 55...tomorrow.

"Are you having a party...or something?" Taylor gasped.

"No...Cynthia quietly replied. "But we could if you want!"

"It would be kind of odd to have a party for someone who's dead," Taylor blissfully responded,. "I would have loved to celebrate all his birthdays...and to have him with us...to get to know him...but that's impossible" she sobbed, then went to her room.

"I didn't mean to upset her with this birthday idea," Cynthia assured her mother-in-law "Everyone knows that my husband Howard, your son--was killed in an industrial accident when she was just three years old. She's not blaming the company. It has provided for me and her since that awful day."

Helen didn't need to hear again how her son was killed. She excused herself.

"Good luck with the cake, hon, but I've got to go," Helen gestured, wiping a tear or two from her eyes. "Tell Taylor I said good-bye. Tell her to call me when she's up to it."

Helen had lost her husband Henry when he was killed in a railroad accident.

Recalling what she read about family life during the early years of the Western Reserve, Helen decided to take another look at what kind of pensions, if any, were available to widows in the early 1800s.

According to one writer, when the War of 1812 was officially over, pensions for soldiers were filed in two different ways.

The first series of pensions were filed in what is known

as "the Old Wars" which is composed of pensions from the Revolutionary War until the end of the Civil War. Most pensions for the War of 1812 are filed in the second series. Both series are located at the National Archives. The acts of 1871 and 1878 that led to the creation of the second series stipulate that the soldier must have served a minimum of 60 days according to the act of 1871 and then later amended to a minimum 14 days in 1878.

Each entry includes names, and if the pension was located in the "Old Wars" series. Other information varies, but most entries include a spouse (at time they are widows filing a pension), where they served, where they lived, and when they were married. The reason for including marriage information is that one of the stipulations for widows filing pensions is they had to be married to the soldier before 1815.

"This is definitely worth looking into" Helen whispered to herself. "Why can't we find anything about John or Teresa?"

Widows eligible for one of those pensions in the early-1880s were tempted to leave the Reserve because of a Typhoid epidemic that was killing people and a naval battle that was raging on their doorstep, Helen read.

The Battle of Lake Erie, sometimes called the Battle of Put-in-Bay, was fought on September 10, 1813 not far from Cleveland. Nine vessels of the United States Navy defeated and captured six vessels of the British Royal Navy.   T h i s ensured American control of the lake for the rest of the war, which in turn allowed the Americans to recover Detroit and win the Battle of the Thames to break the Indian confederation of Tecumseh. It was one of the biggest naval battles of the War of 1812.

Helen took notes on how the Western Reserve continued to grow as canals and railroads brought prosperity to the area.

With the addition of more settlers, there was a need for a steady supply of food and building materials.Travel over mud-soaked mountain roads made the trip from the East too slow to be competitive with lake routes.

City and state leaders saw what was happening with a canal linking the Hudson River to the Great Lakes and sent representatives to survey a route for a canal connecting Lake Erie with the Ohio River. They found it would cost much more than they could afford but had potential for making a profit. They argued that Ohio must find an outlet or perish from stagnation. After a controversial decision choosing Cleveland as the northern terminal of the proposed Ohio-Erie Canal, they borrowed the money and began construction in 1825.

The canal opened with much fanfare in 1827. It turned out to be profitable, but the canal was erroneously blamed for a Typhoid epidemic in the city and railroads were beginning to take their business. In that year the Baltimore & Ohio was said to be the first railroad to operate with a steam locomotive built in the United States.

The main section of the 333-mile Ohio Canal is the 38-mile stretch along the Cuyahoga River from Akron to Cleveland. A series of locks drop canal boats down a 400-foot difference in elevation between the two cities. Most of the canal is still intact as a museum piece and is part of the Cuyahoga Valley National Park. The park includes a Towpath Trail that runs most of its 21 miles along the Cuyahoga River.

Helen made a note to remind herself to ask Taylor what she thought about making a trip on the towpath and went back to searching for information about her widowed sister.

Railroads, she discovered, also made a large contribution to the Western Reserve's emergence as a transportation center and eventually provided widows of employees with benefits unmatched by other industries.

In 1841, there were only thirty-six miles of railroad in Ohio. A group of men from Sandusky called their enterprise the Mad River and Lake Erie Railroad. The construction was crude. The rails were sawed white oak with thin straps of iron spiked to the surface. More than one journalist reported that Cleveland waited another seven years before the first train entered the city.

When settlers in the Reserve caught on to the use of coal to heat their homes, the canals were busy hauling coal from nearby mines. Planners took their time getting approval to to build a rail line from Cleveland to Pittsburgh, where coal was plentiful.

During a debate on the merits of a proposed railroad, one Ohio city is reported to have banned debate with this statement: "If God had designed that his intelligent creatures should travel at a frightful rate of fifteen miles an hour by steam, he would have told it through His holy pamphlet. It is a device of Satan to lead immortal souls down to Hell."

Helen wondered what those folks would have thought after hearing about trains that travel at speeds over 100 miles per hour...and deliver passengers safely to their destinations... or airplanes that fly coast-to-coast at 600 miles per hour...or spacecraft that has taken astronauts to the moon and back.

Back in the1840s, when railroads centered in Cleveland began to crisscross the state, a new industry was born...but without a woman's touch, Helen explained.

Among the first rail lines constructed in the state, all but a few chose a standard axle length (the distance between tracks) at four feet, eight and a half inches. Other early roads choose gauges that ranged up to six feet across, creating chaos at meeting points. Eventually, they all accepted the standard gauge. Before the Civil War stopped construction, Ohio had 2,788 miles of railroad. No other state had so much.

It is not hard to imagine how much our country depended on railroads for building a nationwide system essential to development of industrial sites like the Western Reserve and the defense effort during the Civil War and two World Wars.

One writer described the expansion of railroads as "wealth rolled in on iron wheels."

Many railroads didn't last very long, Helen discovered. Before the national highway system was built In the 1950s, there were around 1,500,000 employees working on 113 Class I railroads. In recent years, after mergers, changes in crew sizes and technical advances, employment has dropped to about 153,000. There were many men--and women--working on the sometimes hazardous railroads that took its toll in deaths and injuries.

Fortunately, railroad employees also have the advantage of a pension program that provides benefits to retired employees, their spouses, widows and young children.

Under the Railroad Retirement Act, the spouse of a retired railroad employee may qualify for an annuity based on the employee's rail service. Lump-sum death benefits may also be payable to qualified survivors.

Among scribes who learned firsthand from survivors of the great migration to the Western Reserve were men like Harvey Rice, who wrote in the 1880s about the experiences of "brave men and resolute women" who sought a land of promise along the shores of Lake Erie.

Rice, a direct descendant of Edmund Rice, an English immigrant, and wife Fannie, had four children. After her death, he married Emma Fitch. They had five children. For his support of education in Cleveland, an elementary school was named in his honor in 1899.

In his comments on Cleveland in 1800, Rice wrote: The unhealthfulness of the locality had induced a removal to more elevated lands in the vicinity. But few, except the family of Lorenzo Carter, remained. Year after year now elapsed with but slight accessions to the population of Cleveland. Numbers of her most enterprising citizens moved to Newburgh, where existed an excellent waterpower, and where the atmosphere, as they believed, was more salubrious. These advantages induced them to think that Newburgh, instead of Cleveland, was destined to become the great metropolis of the Reserve.

The choice seemed inevitable as Welsh, Irish, Polish, German and Czech mill workers poured in to replace English settlers.

Newburgh at that time, was a broad area south of Cleveland that later was split by the county into separate villages that included Garfield Heights; Cuyahoga Heights; Newburgh Heights and a few other townships. Cleveland, which had an elaborate celebration of its 100th anniversary in 1896, eventually was chosen as the county seat.

Many of the early immigrants who came to America chose Newburgh to build their homes. They did their best to preserve traditions and religious beliefs observed in their home countries by clustering nationalities in neighborhoods...neighborhoods recognized for their churches, schools, stores, clothes...and often, the language,too. The mostly Catholic migrants built churches-that drew parishioners from all over the city.

The increase in Catholic migrants led to the creation of the Diocese of Cleveland in 1847 and construction of the Cathedral of St. John the Evangelist in the downtown area. There was a great deal more for Helen to read about when it came to religion and ethnicity in the Western Reserve.

History covers the search for religious freedom by English and German immigrants from early colonial days. Settlers in several of the thirteen colonies wished to practice their own religion. The Massachusetts Bay Colony was established by English Puritans (Congregationalists), Pennsylvania by British Quakers, Maryland by English Catholics, and Virginia by English Anglicans. Despite these, and as a result of intervening religious strife and preference in England, the Plantation Act of 1740 would set official policy for new immigrants coming to British America until the American Revolution.

The text of the First Amendment to the country's Constitution states that "Congress shall make no law respecting an establishment of religion, or prohibiting the free exercise thereof; or abridging the freedom of speech, or of the press; or the right of the people peaceably to assemble, and to petition the Government for a redress of grievances." It guarantees the free exercise of religion while also preventing the government from establishing a state religion.

Few Americans are aware of the colonies' hostility toward Catholics by the 1700s. By this time the penal code against Catholics included test oaths administered to keep Catholics out of office, legislation that barred Catholics from entering certain professions (such as Law), and measures had been enacted to make them incapable of inheriting or purchasing land. By 1718 the ballot had been denied to Catholics in Maryland, following the example of the other colonies, and parents could even be fined for sending children abroad to be educated as Catholics.

The Christian population now comprises the majority of popular religions in the United States. According to the Association of Statisticians of American Religious Bodies, Christians were the largest religious population in all 3,143 counties in the country. Roughly 46.5% of Americans are Protestants, 20.8% are Catholics, 1.6% are Mormons (the name commonly used to refer to members of The Church of the Latter-day Saints, and 1.7% have affiliations with various other Christian denominations.

The Western Reserve in northeastern Ohio remains one of the most ethnically and religiously diverse regions in North America. People migrated to this area from New England and other states, Canada, and from European countries for a variety of reasons. Beginning in the mid-nineteenth century, Cleveland became one of America's prime industrial centers, providing employment to many people of different ethnic and religious backgrounds.

Helen was told that numerous genealogical and historical resources are available for locating residents in northeast Ohio.

A 2015 study estimates there are some 450,000 Christian

believers from a Muslim background in the country, most of them belonging to some form of Protestantism. In 2010 there were approximately 180,000 Arab Americans and about 130,000 Iranian Americans who converted from Islam to Christianity. Dudley Woodbury, a Fulbright scholar of Islam, estimates that 20,000 Muslims convert to Christianity annually in the United States.

There was a time when church records--births, marriages, deaths--was the only source of proof for families looking up their ancestors. Federal, military, state and county records--and the aid of a computer--has made the search more convenient but exhausting.

Helen was getting tired of searching for the Townsends, so she took a break and called her granddaughter to see how she was doing. Taylor's mother answered. "I don't know where she is right now...I think she took a ride on her bike."

"How amazing!" Helen exclaimed. "I was just reading about the Towpath Trail along the canal and wondered if Taylor might be interested in joining me on a little trip. Will you tell her I called?" "Sure!" Cynthia curtly replied...as if something was bothering her.

She didn't mention to Helen that she had received a report from the steel mill raising suspicion about the cause of her husband's death. Her hands trembled as she read it again. They wanted to see if she knew of anyone unrelated to the company who might be responsible. It was obvious she had something to hide.

Taylor had been searching the library for a book about a group of women in Cleveland who were making an effort to record the migration of settlers to the Western Reserve. The Women's Department of the Cleveland Centennial Commission, in preparation for a celebration in 1895, appointed an "historian" to search the history of industrial and philanthropic work engaged by women during the past century.

They found out that every county in the Reserve had already published its history but noticed how much prominence was given to men, with little or no mention of their wives. or widows. The Reserve encompassed all of the following Ohio counties: Ashtabula; Cuyahoga; Erie and Huron (Fire Lands); Geauga; Lorain; Medina; Portage; Trumbull; and portions of Ashland; Mahoning; Ottawa; Summit and Wayne.

The lack of widow's names hampered the search for relatives who survived the War of 1812. But--according to a report from the Library of Congress--there were forty-nine rather elderly widows who survived until Memorial Day in 1922. The list of names and ages--brought out by examination of the pension rolls--included three centenarians, eight were over ninety; twenty-two were octogenarians;the remainder, with one exception, was over seventy. The husbands of these "1812 widows" served in the militia of thirteen states, including two from Ohio.

They are all gone now, thought Taylor, who wondered how many widows never got the chance to apply for benefits...or how many had been rejected when applications included false information. It was not uncommon for women to use what was called "genealogical gems" to collect a pension based on her husband's service during the War of 1812.

Generally, said the government, if a woman applied for benefits based on her husband's service, she had to prove their marriage and his service (if he had not applied earlier). A man who did not die of his wounds, either during the war or later as a continuance of those wounds, was denied a pension. That didn't stop many of our ancestral grandmothers from trying. Their records tell the story. You may find marriage dates, maiden names, children names. and even sometimes the names of some of the widow's family. She decided to find out what the government says about fraud.

Taylor got on the internet and found a contact at the

45

Department for Work and Pensions who agreed to answer a few questions.

She wanted to know when a person can be accused of fraud. She was told you can commit fraud by either intentionally not reporting a change in your circumstances or being dishonest to get benefits.

She wanted to know what would happen if a person is suspected of fraud. She was told that a person suspected of fraud would be contacted by the Department for Work and Pensions, HM Revenue and Customs, the Service and Personnel and Veterans Agency or the suspect's local authority. A person can also expect a visit by Fraud Investigation Officers (FIOs) or asked to attend an interview to talk about your claim. People who are suspected will get a letter telling them their benefit may be stopped while they are being investigated. The FIO will decide whether to take further action.

"What happens after a benefit fraud investigation?" Taylor wanted to know. She was told If there's evidence you've committed fraud, you'll be told to pay back the overpaid money. One or more of the following may also happen:

You may be taken to court or asked to pay a penalty (between $350 and $5,000) and your benefits may be reduced or stopped.

Your benefits can be reduced or stopped for up to 3 years if you're convicted of benefit fraud. The amount of time they're stopped for depends on how many times you've committed fraud.

Only certain benefits can be reduced or stopped. These are called 'sanctionable benefits'. If you commit fraud on a benefit that can't be reduced or stopped, your other benefits can be reduced instead.

The following benefits can be reduced or stopped if you commit benefit fraud:

Carer's Allowance
Employment and Support Allowance
Housing Benefit
Incapacity Benefit
Income Support
Industrial Death Benefit
Industrial Injuries Disablement Benefit
Injuries Reduced Earnings Allowance
Injuries Retirement Allowance
Industrial Injuries Unemployability Supplement
Jobseeker's Allowance
Severe Disablement Allowance
Pension Credit
Universal Credit
War Disablement Pension
War Widow's Pension
War Pension Unemployability Supplement
War Pension Allowance for Lower Standard of Occupation
Widowed Mother's/Parent's Allowance
Widow's Pension/Bereavement Allowance
Working Tax Credit

CHAPTER V

A NATION DIVIDED

A phone call at four in the morning startled Helen while she was still fast asleep. It was Cynthia. She was crying and wanted to know if Taylor was with her.

"It would be a surprise to me if she were," responded Helen, "but I'll check to see." She went from empty room to empty room, carrying the telephone with her.

Cynthia was still on the line, when Helen was about to report that her daughter was not there and had found a note from the fifteen-year-old girl.

"Gramma," the note began, "don't worry about me but I've decided to look for Aunt Teresa by myself. There is something strange going on here...love you, Taylor."

Helen wondered whether to tell Cynthia about the note and had a hard time imagining why she wanted to continue the search by herself. Helen reminded Cynthia that her daughter got a last-minute invitation to join classmates at a campout this weekend.... "and that's where she probably is," she assured her. The rest of the morning was relatively quiet (pun intended).

"It's obvious that our search has brought unwanted attention from Federal investigators," she thought to herself. "They probably scared the hell out of that poor kid."

She decided to do her shopping and was about to check

out when she spotted a copy of the Harriet Beecher Snowe novel "Uncle Tom's Cabin."

After putting away her groceries, she drove to the Lakeside Park and found a shady spot to relax and read the book. The story depicts the harsh conditions experienced by enslaved African Americans.

The book reached millions as a novel and play. It became influential in the United States and Great Britain, energizing anti-slavery forces in the American north, while provoking widespread anger in the South.

Critics said the emotional portrayal of the effects of slavery on individuals captured the nation's attention. Stowe showed that slavery touched all of society, beyond the people directly involved as masters, traders and slaves. Her novel added to the debate about abolition and slavery, and aroused opposition in the South. In the South, Stowe was depicted as out of touch, arrogant and guilty of slander.

After the Civil War, she campaigned for women's rights, arguing that the position of a married women...is, in many respects, precisely similar to that of the negro slave. She can make no contract and hold no property; whatever she inherits or earns becomes at that moment the property of her husband....Her husband, Calvin Stow, died in 1886. She died. a widow, in 1896 and is buried in Andover, Massachusetts.

Helen read how many of Stowe's abolitionist friends were involved in what was called the "Underground Railroad," ... routes that helped slaves escape to freedom ... routes that went through the Western Reserve...her backyard. She got on the library computer to see if there was any record of relatives who might have participated in the venture.

First, she explored where the name "Underground Railroad" originated. Historians say the first use of the name occurred in the 1830s, long before the first railroads began to operate in America. It was neither a railroad nor was it underground.

When Congress established the Northwest Ordinance in

1787, one of the provisions forbid slavery in any new future state admitted to the Union, north of the Ohio River. Later Congress added to that ordinance a law that made it a federal crime to give aid or harbor escaping slaves that could be punished by severe fines or even imprisonment.

It was under these conditions that caused abolitionists to form secretive networks that could help escaping slaves move along a network that was neither advertised nor written.

Because this activity of helping escaping slaves was against the law and therefore these activities had to be concealed. The term railroad was used because those people involved in the activities used terms commonly associated with railroads, to describe different aspects of their activities.

Slaves were called cargo or **passengers**. Hiding places or safe houses were called **stations.** Guides leading the escaping slaves were called **conductors.** People helping the escaping slaves, but not guiding them, were called **agents.** People providing financial resources for these activities were called **stockholders.**

In Ohio there were 10 exit ports commonly used, with the most often used ports being Toledo, Sandusky, Cleveland, Fairport Harbor, and Ashtabula Harbor. Oberlin was a key junction on the Underground Railroad that connected five different routes escaping slaves could have taken.

The main entry point to Ohio was along the Ohio River and most notably was a small community called Ripley where John Rankin and a small group assisted 1,000s of escaping slaves and started them on their journey.

Among the safe houses on the Underground Railroad familiar to Helen was the Rev. William Hanford House in Hudson. She knew about Rev. Hanford from neighbors, descendants of Rev. Thomas Hanford, who came to America in the 1600s.

Among other safe houses located in Hudson were: The Whedon-Hinsdale House; Spring Hill Farm; Asahel Kilbourne

House; Case-Barlow Farm; Harvey Coe House; Norman Baldwin House; John Brown Tannery House; Elizur Wright Jr. House; Titus Hand House; Brown-Strong House; John Markille; David Hudson House; Old Western Reserve College; George Holccomb/Timothy Hudson House; Original First Congregational Church Building; Kilbourne-Oviatt House; Thirty Acres; Free Congregational Church; Jeremiah Root Brown House; and Lora Case.

In Cleveland, which played a prominent role in the drive toward national emancipation of its enslaved population, stations were located at the Cozad-Bates House; St. John's Episcopal Church; Needham Castle; Plymouth Church, East Cleveland Township Farms, and others.

Helen was overwhelmed by the number of Ohioans who risked their lives to participate in the Underground Railroad. Among them were William Hubbard of Ashtabula, where "night after night conductors landed passengers in his cellar or hayloft..." and Rush R. Sloane, a Sandusky, Ohio, lawyer, and abolitionist who built his home in the early 1850s. The wives and windows who toiled to keep their homes as safe havens for the escaping slaves got little credit for the historic endeavor.

Helen was still sitting at the park, the book folded in her lap, when a young black man in a military uniform approached her and introduced himself. "Private Arnold Hastings, Ma'am... how did you like the book?"

It was either his manner or his looks, but Helen's reaction to the question had her temporarily mystified. "I don't know how to answer," she muttered, "I thought it was kind of sad." Then, asking politely, she asked, "have you been watching me?"

"Only the last couple of minutes, when I saw what you were reading," he explained. "My great-great grandparents traveled on that railroad many years ago...or I wouldn't be here....I've been trying to track them down but I can't find anything...I don't think they kept any records of passengers in those days."

"Please, sit down," Helen begged the soldier. "Are you in a hurry?" she asked. Before he could answer, she jotted down an address from her book.

"Ohio is fortunate to have the National Underground Railroad Freedom Center in Cincinnati," she pointed out. She told him the center provides a clearing house of information about the Underground Railroad and suggested he write to them at Freedom Center; 50 E. Freedom Way, Cincinnati 45202.

"I'll try it," said the soldier, thankful for Helen's help as he tucked the note in his shirt pocket and joined a group of people milling around a picnic table. Helen headed for home, eager to see what's new with her granddaughter.

She had several messages on her phone...one from her daughter-in-law Cynthia, one from her granddaughter Taylor and a third one from a government investigator. Cynthia was still worried about her missing daughter. Taylor is with neighbors down the street and the G-man has an important question for her.

All of those can wait, she decided, as she opened her mail. Beside the usual bills and advertisements was a letter from the Veteran's Administration asking for information about Phillip Townsend. "Strange!" she thought, "why is the VA asking me about a missing in-law...shouldn't they have a record on him?"

Helen was unable to console Cynthia. She was in tears despite being assured that Taylor was safe and not in any kind of trouble...for now, anyway.

"What next?" she thought, raising her voice in an otherwise empty house. Any effort to locate Teresa and find John Townsend's record among soldiers killed in action seemed to alienate half the family, while the other half refused to quit.

It was, in a way, similar to the dispute over slavery that split the nation and led to the War Between the States. Historians say the causes of the Civil War can be traced back to tensions formed early in the nation's history. While the issue of slavery was at the heart of the division between North and South, a complex array of issues led to the South's secession. The war lasted from 1861 to 1865 and led to over 618,000 casualties, many from Ohio and the Western Reserve.

Helen was trying to decide to make that call to the Veteran's Administration when a car pulled into the driveway...and she saw her granddaughter tumbling out. She was wrestling with a knapsack, blanket and a pile of books and looked a little disheveled.

"Hi gram!" she cowered. "Can I come in?"

The only thing Helen could say at that moment was "where have you been and why haven't you called your mother?"

Ignoring the admonition, Taylor heaved her knapsack on the front porch, dropped the books, tossed the blanket on top, and rushed to give her gramma a big hug.

They stood in a silent embrace for half a minute, then spoke with their eyes.

"Leave that stuff here for a moment," Helen implored, "Get in here, wash up and we'll get you something to eat ."

"Oh thank you gramma," replied Taylor, "I've got a lot to tell you."

Sitting across from her at the kitchen table, she began with "My father's death was no accident...his coworkers think he was murdered."

"Where did you get that?" gulped Helen.

Taylor explained that she had been camping with kids whose fathers worked with her father at the time of his death. "They insisted he was much too careful to overlook loose bolts and loose fittings while hanging fifty feet in the air...they think someone loosened the bolts on purpose, causing him to fall."

"But the company conceded to a settlement after a thorough investigation," Helen mildly argued. "Who would have done such a thing...and why?"

The two sat for a while...stunned...trying to figure out if

53

the accusation had any merit, wondering what to tell Taylor's widowed mother, wondering if she had anything to do with it.

The mailman roused them from their stupor when he shuffled up the front steps and dropped off a large envelope from the Veteran's Administration. In it was a letter of explanation and a printout of men and women named Townsend who had a record of service beginning with the War of 1812. It also contained similar records of Beck and Hanford veterans from the Civil War and more recent military action around the world.

Not much about widows or pensions.

"Wow...this will keep us busy for a while," remarked a reinvigorated Taylor, who began leafing through Civil War records. Helen cautioned her to hold off until they could review the history of the war.

"What's the hurry?" asked Helen, as she hunted and found "American History" in Taylor's stack of books. They sat together to take a look.

Both were aware that the bombardment of Fort Sumter near Charleston, South Carolina on April 12, 1861 was the beginning of the Civil War. They read about the war between the states lasting from 1861 to 1865 and how it led to over 650,000 casualties. Although slavery was at the heart of the division between North and South, the book described other issues that led to the South's secession.

The invention of the cotton gin in 1793 made growing cotton very profitable. The machine was able to reduce the time it took to separate seeds from the cotton. It encouraged Southern growers to switch from other crops to cotton, creating a one-crop economy dependent on slavery.

The Northern states, which focused on industrialization, had a different attitude about slavery.

This disparity between the two regions of the country set up a major difference in economic attitudes. The South was based on the plantation system while the North was focused on city life. This change in the North meant that society evolved as people of different cultures and classes had to work together. The South continued to hold onto an antiquated social order. On both sides, economics influenced people's political views.

Some people argued for greater rights for the states and others argued that the federal government needed to have more control. During attempts to resolve differences on state rights, Northerners became more polarized against slavery. Many in the North came to view slavery as not just socially unjust, but morally wrong.

The presidential election of 1860 would be the deciding point for the Union. Even though things were already near a boiling point after Lincoln was elected, South Carolina issued its "Declaration of the Causes of Secession" on December 24, 1860. They believed that Lincoln was anti-slavery and in favor of Northern interests.

President Buchanan's administration did little to quell the tension or stop what would become known as "Secession Winter." Between election day and Lincoln's inauguration in March, seven states had seceded from the Union: South Carolina, Mississippi, Florida, Alabama, Georgia, Louisiana, and Texas.

The Civil War consisted of nearly 10,500 battles, engagements, and other military actions including nearly 50 major battles and about 100 others that had major significance. The remainder were skirmishes, reconnaissances, naval engagements, sieges, bombardments, etc. The engagements were fought in 23 different states.

The war, however, did not officially conclude at Appomattox, a tiny village west of Petersburg, Virginia. But what happened there marked the beginning of the end for the Confederacy.

After the fall of Richmond, the Confederate capital, on April 2, 1865, officials in the Confederate government, including President Jefferson Davis, fled. The dominoes began to fall.

The surrender at Appomattox took place a week later on April 9.

While it was the most significant surrender to take place during the Civil War, Gen. Robert E. Lee, the Confederacy's most respected commander, surrendered only his Army of Northern Virginia to Union Gen. Ulysses S. Grant.

Several other Confederate forces—some large units, some small, had yet to surrender before President Andrew Johnson could declare that the Civil War was officially over.

The Grant-Lee agreement served not only as a signal that the South had lost the war but also as a model for the rest of the surrenders that followed.

After Richmond fell and Davis fled, Confederate commanders were on their own to surrender their commands to Union forces. Surrenders, paroles, and amnesty for many Confederate combatants would take place over the next several months and into 1866 throughout the South and border states.

Not until 16 months after Appomattox, on August 20, 1866, did the President formally declare an end to the war.

Nearly 320,000 Ohioans served in the Union army, more than any other northern state except New York and Pennsylvania. Of these, 5,092 were free blacks. Ohio had the highest percentage of population enlisted in the military of any state. Sixty percent of all the men between the ages of 18 and 45 were in the service. Ohio mustered 230 regiments of infantry and cavalry, as well as 26 light artillery batteries and 5 independent companies of sharpshooters. Total casualties among these units numbered 35,475 men, more than 10% of all the Buckeyes in uniform during the war. There were 6,835 men killed in action, including 402 officers.

Helen described the monument in Cleveland honoring Civil War soldiers and sailors. Located in the southeast quadrant of Public Square in downtown Cleveland is the huge Soldiers' and Sailors' Monument which opened on July 4, 1894.

It consists of a 125-foot black Quincy granite shaft erected on a square base constructed of roughhewn granite blocks trimmed in sandstone and housing a memorial building. On its elevated base stands a sequence of larger than life bronze sculptures depicting soldiers and sailors in battle. Inside the memorial building are a series of marble tablets listing 9,000 Civil War veterans that served with Cuyahoga County regiments or were from Cuyahoga County.

During the American Civil War, Ohio played a key role in providing troops, military officers, and supplies to the Union army. Numerous leading generals and army commanders hailed from Ohio. The General-in-Chief of the Union armies, Ulysses S. Grant, was born in Clermont County in 1822. Among the 19 major generals from Ohio were William T. Sherman, Philip H. Sheridan, Don Carlos Buell, Jacob D. Cox, George Cook, George Armstrong Custer, James A. Garfield, Irvin McDowell, James B. McPherson, William S. Rosecrans, and Alexander M. McCook.

In addition to Grant and Garfield, three other Ohio Civil War veterans would become President of the United States in the decades following the war: William McKinley of Canton, Rutherford B.Hayes of Fremont and Benjamin Harrison of the greater Cincinnati area.

Among the 320,000 veterans from Ohio who served in the war was Congressional Medal of Honor recipient Private Edward Raymond Hanford. Private Hanford was born in Ohio in 1845 and grew up in Allegany County, New York. Although only 16, he enlisted as a private in the 93rd New York volunteer Infantry and later transferred to the Second U.S. Cavalry.

He was enlisted into Company H by regimental adjutant James McQuesten at Harpers Ferry, Virginia on October 22, 1862. Private Hanford served as a private through all of the grueling campaigns of 1863 and most of 1864 without incident or wound. This changed in the Shenandoah Valley on October 9, 1864 during fighting near Woodstock, Virginia, or the "Woodstock Races," as they became known to the Cavalry Corps of the Army of the Potomac.

Private Hanford captured the flag of the 32d Battalion Virginia Cavalry in hand to hand fighting. In General Orders dated October 14, 1864, Hanford was awarded the Medal of Honor for extraordinary heroism. Private Hanford was discharged from the army at the expiration of his term of service at Hagerstown, Maryland on January 31,1865. After the war, he moved to Calaveras County, California where he worked as a miner.

Both Helen and Taylor were excited to learn that a distant relative of the Hanford family had been awarded the Medal of Honor. They wondered if anyone had bothered to look up any relatives that served in the Civil War....and if so...what did they find out?

They stopped what they were doing to visit Julia Hanford, an elderly neighbor and widow who lost her husband in World War II. To their dismay, Julia, at first, didn't have any idea what they were talking about...but then remembered a note about a stack of letters saved by her husband's grandfather. The note listed names of soldiers who were exchanging letters with nieces in Delaware County, New York between 1862 and 1865. Their names, all Hanford's who served in the 144th New York Voluntary Infantry during the Civil War, were quickly copied.

Here's a partial list of Hanford men who fought in the Civil War:

State	Name	Unit
Massachusetts	Albert Hanford	3rd Massachusetts Heavy Artillery
New York	Andrew Hanford	12th New York Cavalry
Wisconsin	Arthur Hanford	3rd Wisconsin Infantry

New York	Augustus E. Hanford	18th New York Infantry
Connecticut	Augustus Hanford	23rd Connecticut Infantry
Connecticut	Benjamin F. Hanford	28th Connecticut Infantry
Michigan	Benjamin F. Hanford	16th Michigan Infantry
New York	Carroll A. Hanford	144th New York Infantry
New York	Cephas Hanford	5th, 140th & 13th New York Infantry
Illinois Artillery	Charles C. Hanford	Mercantile Battery, Illinois Light
Ohio	Charles C. Hanford	14th Ohio Infantry
Connecticut	Charles Hanford	14th Connecticut Infantry
Kansas	Charles Hanford	6th Kansas Cavalry
New York	Charles Hanford	3rd New York Cavalry & 143rd Infantry
New York	Charles I. Hanford	87th New York Infantry
New York	Chas. N. Hanford	90th New York Infantry
New York	Chauncey D. Hanford	144th New York Infantry

They thanked Julia and promised to get back if they get more information about her in-laws family. In the meantime, they planned to explore the roll of women in the Civil War.

CHAPTER VI

THE FORGOTTEN WOMAN

Once they had a better picture of the number of men who served in the Civil War, Helen and her granddaughter got busy searching records of women who served their country.

Curled up on her living room couch looking through history books, Helen couldn't help to notice how historians made little effort to credit women for their role in creating a new nation. In her opinion, from the time the first Pilgrims came ashore at Plymouth to the launching of space travel, women haven't been recognized for their contribution to the country.

"Where should we start?" Taylor asked her grandmother.

"That's easy," responded Helen. "Among the earliest events recorded was the transformation of the Western Reserve. That 120-mlle strip of vacant land in Northeastern Ohio provided a homestead for hundreds of immigrants anxious to escape British domination. The problem was getting there. The women suffered agonizing hardship as they trekked ten or fifteen miles a day behind horses and ox-drawn wagons over 450 miles of mountainous wilderness to reach their destination."

"I can't imagine what that was like...hiking through dense woods in all kinds of weather...fighting off indians...running into British patrols. How did they make it?" shrugged Taylor.

"Determination and guts," guessed her grandmother.

"From what I read many of those immigrants died on their way and were buried where they died. There was no turning back. Women and children were the most vulnerable but some men didn't make it either."

Helen read a few of the reports.

Those families that got to their designated homestead had to build a cabin, prepare gardens and store food. There were no stores and the closest neighbor could be five miles away. Indians were always a problem. What had been their property was now being invaded by strangers and they were angry.

Occasionly, especially in areas close to a salt spring, they would kill the settlers and burn their cabins. The War of 1812 chased most of the Indians and British from the Reserve, sparking a flood of immigrants to the area.

With the outbreak of war in 1861, women and men alike eagerly volunteered to fight for the cause. Women played many roles in the Civil War. They did not sit idly by waiting for the men in their lives to come home from the battlefield. Whatever their duties were, these new jobs redefined their traditional roles as housewives and mothers and made them an important part of the war effort.

In the years before the Civil War, the lives of American women were shaped by a set of ideals that historians call "the Cult of True Womanhood." "True women" devoted their lives to creating a clean, comfortable, nurturing home for their husbands and children.

Many women supported the war effort as nurses and aides, while others took a more upfront approach and secretly enlisted in the army or served as spies and smugglers.

This conventional picture of gender roles during the Civil War does not tell the entire story. Men were not the only ones to fight that war. Women bore arms and charged into battle, too. Like the men, there were women who lived in camp, suffered in prisons, and died for their respective causes.

Images of women during that conflict center on

self-sacrificing nurses, romantic spies, or brave ladies maintaining the home front in the absence of their men. The men, of course, marched off to war, lived in germ-ridden camps, engaged in heinous battle, languished in appalling prison camps, and died horribly, yet heroically.

Both the Union and Confederate armies forbade the enlistment of women. Women soldiers of the Civil War therefore assumed masculine names, disguised themselves as men, and hid the fact they were female. Because they passed as men, it is impossible to know with any certainty how many women soldiers served in the Civil War. Estimates place as many as 250 women in the ranks of the Confederate army.

Someone has stated the number of women soldiers known to the service as little less than four hundred. There were soldiers who were convinced that a larger number of women disguised themselves and enlisted in the service, for one cause or other, than was dreamed of. Entrenched in secrecy, and regarded as men, they were sometimes revealed as women, by accident or casualty. Some startling histories of these military women were current in the gossip of army life.

Soldiers in the Union army were not the only ones who knew of soldier-women. Ordinary citizens heard of them, too. Mary Owens, discovered to be a woman after she was wounded in the arm, returned to her Pennsylvania home to a warm reception and press coverage. She had served for eighteen months under the alias John Evans.

In the post - Civil War era, the topic of women soldiers continued to arise in both literature and the press. Frank Moore's Women of the War, published in 1866, devoted an entire chapter to the military heroines of the North. A year later, L. P. Brockett and Mary Vaughan mentioned ladies "who from whatever cause . . . donned the male attire and concealed their sex . . . [who] did not seek to be known as women, but preferred to pass for men."... Loretta Velazquez published her memoirs in 1876. She served the Confederacy as Lt. Harry

Buford, a self-financed soldier not officially attached to any regiment.

The existence of soldier-women was no secret during or after the Civil War. The reading public, at least, was well aware that these women rejected Victorian social constraints confining them to the domestic sphere. Their motives were open to speculation, perhaps, but not their actions, as numerous newspaper stories and obituaries of women soldiers testified.

Most of the articles provided few specific details about the individual woman's army career. For example, the obituary of Satronia Smith Hunt merely stated she enlisted in an Iowa regiment with her first husband. He died of battle wounds, but she apparently emerged from the war unscathed.

An 1896 story about Mary Stevens Jenkins, who died in 1881, tells an equally brief tale. She enlisted in a Pennsylvania regiment when still a schoolgirl, remained in the army two years, received several wounds, and was discharged without anyone ever realizing she was female. The press seemed unconcerned about the women's actual military exploits. Rather, the fascination lay in the simple fact that they had been in the army.

The army itself, however, held no regard for women soldiers, Union or Confederate. Indeed, despite recorded evidence to the contrary, the U.S. Army tried to deny that women played a military role, however small,

In the Northern states, women organized ladies' aid societies to supply the Union troops with everything they needed, from food (they baked and canned and planted fruit and vegetable gardens for the soldiers) to clothing (they sewed and laundered uniforms, `knitted socks and gloves, mended blankets and embroidered quilts and pillowcases) to cash (they organized door-to-door fundraising campaigns, county fairs and performances of all kinds to raise money for medical supplies and other necessities).

63

"That's enough for today," Helen sighed, slamming the cover on her notepad.

"We've spent the entire afternoon reading and talking about women's role in the Civil War. It's getting late and I should be getting you home." She suggested they put down the books and talk about what she is going to tell her mother when she gets home.

"My mother will not believe anything I tell her," Taylor emphasized.

"Then show her this," insisted Helen as she handed her a copy of the government handout on "Benefit Fraud."

"Oh...that's gonna go over like a lead balloon," Taylor predicted. "I've got some other stuff she might be interested in."

With that she showed Helen a collection of material from the U.S. Census Bureau that shows the marital status of the population by sex and age, widow statistics from the Bureau, the effects of widowhood, and some stories about the worst countries in the world to be a woman today.

"Well, if you don't mind," Helen pleaded as she slipped on her jacket, "I would like to see those reports, too."

Taylor just happened to have an extra copy, which she was eager to share.

Given top priority was a report by the U.S. Census Bureau on the number of widowers in the U.S. and a list of potential effects experienced by widows and widowers.

According to the U.S. Census Bureau there were 800,000 new widows/widowers in the U.S. in 2002. Nearly 700,000 women lose their husbands each year and will be widows for an average of 14 years.

Marital Status of the Population by Sex and Age

Sex and age	Number of persons (1,000) In thousands

(202 represents 202,000)

Male	
18 to 19 years old	2
20 to 24 years old	-
25 to 29 years old	14
30 to 34 years old	21
35 to 39 years old	21
40 to 44 years old	67
45 to 54 years old	202
55 to 64 years old	292
65 to 74 years old	726
75 years old and over	1347

Female	
18 to 19 years old	-
20 to 24 years old	16
25 to 29 years old	36
30 to 34 years old	58
35 to 39 years old	134
40 to 44 years old	185
45 to 54 years old	640
55 to 64 years old	1487
65 to 74 years old	2888
75 years old and over	5844

According to the American Association of Retired Persons (AARP),there are 13.6 million widows in the United States. Over 11 million of the widowed, in the US, are women. The statistics show more than numbers:

According to a study launched by Cherie Blair, wife of the former British prime minister, at least least 245 million women around the world have been widowed and more than 115 million of them live in devastating poverty, According to the report, the countries with the highest number of widows in 2010 were China with 43 million, India with 42.4 million, the United States with 13.6 million, Indonesia with 9.4 million, Japan with 7.4 million, Russia with 7.1 million, Brazil with 5.6 million, Germany with 5.1 million, and Bangladesh and Vietnam with about 4.7 million each.

Another study ranks death of a spouse number one on a stress index scale; making this one of life's most devastating events.

Widows and the friends and family that love them are aware of the snowball effect of those who lose a spouse or significant other. As many as 60% of widows will experience a serious illness in the 12 months following that loss. Those widowed have reported illnesses like cancer, pancreas' shutting down, shingles....

Sleep can be severely impacted with the loss of a spouse. Disrupted sleep makes it harder to handle our grief, our lives, and even the day-to-day duties of making the bed or paying the bills. And it may also affect our health.

Widowhood is said to increase a survivors' risk of dying. A study of nearly 400,000 elderly American couples shows that the effect of widowhood on mortality varies substantially by the causes of death of both spouses.Widowhood increases survivors' risk of dying from almost all causes, including cancer, but it increases the risk for some causes more than for others.

On average 75% of the survivor's support base is lost following the loss of a spouse or significant other; this includes loss of support from family and friends. There are a multitude of reasons for losing friends and family including; loss of couples friends. Those widowed can isolate, we can be sad and unpleasant to be around. Family members are grieving and they go through the unpleasant stages of grief.

People who feel consistently lonely have a 14% higher risk of premature death than those who don't, a new study shows. The impact of loneliness on early death is almost as strong as being poor, which increased the chances of dying early by 19% the research found.

Between 5% and 7.5% of all children are said to be actively grieving.

"Almost half the women over 65 years of age in the United States are widows. About 7 in 10 of these women live alone." (U.S. Census, 2000) In recent years the average American woman's expected lifespan has increased to eighty or more. However, the societal systems in place for caring for the elderly have not changed at the same rapid pace leaving many widows in poverty.

One Social Security Administration report shows that "for the past thirty or more years the rate of poverty among elderly widows is consistently three to four times higher than elderly married women." These statistics do not take into account the population of widows under the age of 65 or those raising families.

The image of the 21st century woman is confident, prosperous, glowing with health and beauty.But for many of the 3.3 billion female occupants of our planet, the perks of the cyber age never arrived. Women continue to feel the age-old lash of violence, repression, isolation, enforced ignorance and discrimination.

"These things are universal," says Taina Bien-Aime, executive director of New York-based Equality Now. "There is not one single country where women can feel absolutely safe."

In spite of real progress in women's rights around the globe – better laws, political participation, education and income – the bedrock problems that have dogged women for centuries remain. Even in wealthy countries, there are pockets of private pain where women are unprotected and under attack.

Some countries, often the poorest and most conflict-ridden, have a level of violence that makes life unbearable for women. Richer ones may burden them with repressive laws, or sweep the problems of the least advantaged under the carpet. In any country, refugee women are among the most vulnerable.

So widespread are the disadvantages that it's hard to pinpoint the worst places in the world for women. Some surveys rate their problems by quality of life, others by health indicators. Human rights groups point to countries where violations are so severe that even murder is routine.

Following are some of the worst countries to be a woman today:

Afghanistan: The average Afghan girl will live to only 45 – one year less than an Afghan male. After three decades of war and religion-based repression, an overwhelming number of women are illiterate. More than half of all brides are under 16, and one woman dies in childbirth every half hour. Domestic violence is so common that 87 per cent of women admit to experiencing it. But more than one million widows are on the streets, often forced into prostitution. Afghanistan is the only country in which the female suicide rate is higher than that of males.

Democratic Republic of Congo: In the eastern DRC, a war that claimed more than 3 million lives has ignited again, with women on the front line. Rapes are so brutal and systematic that UN investigators have called them unprecedented. Many victims die; others are infected with HIV and left to look after children alone. Foraging for food and water exposes women to yet more violence. Without money, transport or connections, they have no way of escape.

Iraq: The U.S.-led invasion to "liberate" Iraq from Saddam Hussein has imprisoned women in an inferno of sectarian violence that targets women and girls. The literacy rate, once the highest in the Arab world, is now among the lowest as families fear risking kidnapping and rape by sending girls to school.

Nepal: Early marriage and childbirth exhaust the country's malnourished women, and one in 24 will die in pregnancy or childbirth. Daughters who aren't married off may be sold to traffickers before they reach their teens. Widows face extreme abuse and discrimination if they're labelled bokshi, meaning witches. A low-level civil war between government and Maoist rebels has forced rural women into guerrilla groups.

Sudan: While Sudanese women have made strides under reformed laws, the plight of those in Darfur, in western Sudan, has worsened. Abduction, rape or forced displacement have destroyed more than 1 million women's lives since 2003.

Other countries in which women's lives are significantly worse than men's include Guatemala, where an impoverished female underclass faces domestic violence. An epidemic of gruesome unsolved murders has left hundreds of women dead, some of their bodies left with hate messages.

In Mali, one of the world's poorest countries, few women escape the torture of genital mutilation, many are forced into early marriages, and one in 10 dies in pregnancy or childbirth.

In the tribal border areas of Pakistan, women are gang-raped as punishment for men's crimes. But honor killing is more widespread, and a renewed wave of religious extremism is targeting female politicians, human rights workers and lawyers.

In the Somali capital, Mogadishu, a vicious civil war has put women, who were the traditional mainstay of the family, under attack. In a society that has broken down, women are exposed daily to rape, dangerously poor health care for pregnancy, and attack by armed gangs.

The reports were giving Taylor a lot to think about.

She had hoped that Cynthia, who was content with the settlement of her husbands "accidental" death, may be ready to loosen up when talking about her Aunt Teresa.

Taylor was silent, deep in thought, as Helen drove her home. A light rain was falling and a strange dark-colored car was in the driveway. It had a police license plate.

"Looks like my mother has company," Taylor surmised. I wonder what's up?"

"I better go with you," Helen volunteered. "Looks like your mother might need some help."

They were met at the door by a husky officer in plain clothes who asked: "Are you Helen Beck...Teresa Townsend's sister?"

"Yes," she hastily responded, and asked "What's going on?"

"Sorry to tell you...your sister is dead," he bluntly declared.

"How? Why? Where? questioned the distraught Helen, who walked in on the detectives examination.

"We got a call from a neighbor who detected a foul odor coming out of your sister's home...and from the Post Office when mail started piling up," he began. "We broke in to find her deteriorating body lying on a bed. We found a couple of names and addresses, including yours, but decided to stop here first," he told Helen.

"Now you tell me!...if this woman is your sister, how come you didn't know she was dead?"

Helen looked around and saw Cynthia sitting in a recliner, swabbing a handkerchief across her face--bloodshot eyes staring at her from behind a blank expression. "We, my granddaughter and I, have been looking for her for several months...her grandson Bill insisted we leave them alone...he said he was taking care of her."

"Well, he took care of her all right," said the policeman..."there's not a penny left in the house...no bank account, nothing of value, no papers,except for this list with your names...and he's gone."

"Are you aware that Federal investigators are looking into the possibility of fraud in this case?" Helen asked.

"Yep," he replied. "Her husband was a helicopter pilot shot down in Vietnam. A couple years ago his widow's death benefits were unlawfully directed to another person and the payments were temporarily suspended."

"That's not all of it," snapped Helen, "We just learned that Cynthia's husband Howard found out who did this and was ready to turn him in when he was killed in an industrial accident...an accident former co-workers suspect was intentional murder. There is a Federal investigation of the whole thing going on right now."

"Where is this grandson?" the detective asked.

"Probably with Philip," Taylor piped up, "that's his father-- Philip Townsend--a guy who abandoned his family years ago, changed his name and just dropped off the earth."

With that, the detective got on his phone and asked his captain to alert the Federal investigators about Teresa's death and the possibility of charging someone with murder.

POLICE INTENSIFY INVESTIGATION

Helen immediately recalled that Bill had recently told her that Teresa "spends a lot of time in bed, tended by nurses from a nearby health center and regular visits by me and my family, and my two sisters and their families."

He also said arrangements had been made for Teresa's funeral, including a Mass at St. James Church.

"We never did check that out," Helen told the officer, "he insisted we leave her and her family alone...we have been searching ancestral records of her and her husband ever since...now this."

"We'll let you know when you can have the funeral," the officer emphasized.

"That poor women," declared Helen, "her son abandoned the family and her grandson leaves her to die alone in that empty house."

When the officer left, Helen drove to the church to see what kind of "funeral arrangements" Bill said were made. It turned out the "arrangements" were made with a private company that no longer existed. All her important papers, including a receipt for the funeral, were gone.

Cynthia was a bundle of nerves. She also suspected that Philip may of had something to do with her husband's death...a something that could jeopardize her settlement with the steel mill...best if she could keep quiet. The company had sent her a letter renewing suspicion about the cause of the accident.

Newspaper articles about Teresa's death helped to alert Bill's sisters--Mary and Anita--to59 police involvement in the case and the pending funeral. They sent letters expressing sympathy and offering to help locate Philip, their father, and Bill, their brother. The letters were referred to investigators preparing for a hearing and the search was on.

Federal investigators found real estate records from more than ten years earlier that showed the sale of a lakeside cabin in West Virginia to a Pat Tordaloni, with no former address. A team of state police, with weapons drawn, surrounded the cabin and called for Bill and Phillip to come out. They surrendered without resistance.

Sitting together in the back seat of a cruiser sent from Cleveland, the two men--father and son--started blaming each other for their predicament.

Philip had made up the name to escape detection but, instead, drew attention. Bill's insistence on being left alone didn't help either. Now both he and his father face prosecution in court.

Before questioning got underway, officials of the steel mill brought in a container of bolts and fastenings that had been retrieved from the "accident" site when Howard Beck was killed. He was preparing to climb a tall ladder to inspect a newly installed device when it came crashing down, knocking him off the ladder. Their staff had determined that someone had turned off the device, loosened and cut the bolts "before" the accident. They gave a brief demonstration of how it could have happened but had no clue who tampered with the device.

In the lawsuit, lawyers argued the device was improperly installed. They won a big settlement. A big chunk of it went to Cynthia.

There were no witnesses to the accident but fellow workers

who knew Howard came forward to describe his passion for safety and his experience on the job. "He never saw it coming," they said. "We think he was murdered."

The hearing then focused on the probability that Teresa'a death was murder. When Bill found the government had sent letters telling family members it was sending an investigator to check on fraud, he collected everything he could lay his hands on and took off--leaving his 93-year-old mother to die.

"There could have been some big money involved here," the detective told the hearing officer. I'll get an order and see what we can find."

After making a few routine phone calls and spending some time on a computer, he confirmed that a death gratuity of $100,000 or more, was payable--under certain conditions--to surviving family members of a member of the armed forces killed in action. "There were also some widow benefits and child care benefits being paid after Teresa took custody of her son's three children, and she was eligible for collecting Social Security. "The problem is," he continued, "whatever benefits that were being paid accumulated in a hefty bank account... that no longer exists."

"What do you mean by hefty?" asked the hearing officer.

"Half a million, give or take a few thousand," he replied.

"All right...we need to get some help here...and find out where that money went! Who else are we seeing here?" he asked.

Sitting on a bench out in the hallway opposite the hearing room, Helen, Cynthia and Bill's two sisters waited for their turn.

"Bring in Mrs. Townsend's sister...Helen Beck, I believe," the hearing officer decided.

"Please, have a seat," he gestured...then introduced himself and gave her a brief description of the pending charges.

I understand you are a widow and that your husband was killed in a railroad accident...is that right?" he started off.

Helen didn't like talking about her husband's death...it

aroused so many memories and was very depressing. All she could do was grunt a "Yes."

"Then you know something about pensions and death benefits..." he continued.

Again, it upset her to talk about it. But, after a moment, she made sure he knew there was a big difference between railroad death and pension benefits, and military death and pension benefits.

"My husband was very frugal," she explained. "He was eligible for railroad benefits but he also took out a substantial life insurance policy that has been very helpful to me."

"Did you know that your sister Teresa was in such bad shape?" the hearing officer asked.

"We were told she was getting care and just wanted to be left alone," Helen explained, "Her son told us she did not want any company...so we gave up looking for her."

"Her son, or maybe her grandson, or both of them may be held responsible for her death," the officer interrupted. "They manipulated a change in her name, gave a false address, took her money and left her. It is one of the worst cases of triple dipping ever seen around here."

I had no idea," Helen said, slumping in her chair. But my husband did...and so did my son. They knew it was perfectly legal to collect on two pensions...but they believed Philip--who hated his job at the steel mill--was secretly negotiating to buy a campsite somewhere in West Virginia. Howard heard Philip mention the place on the telephone."

"So you think your husband knew what Philip was planning to do with that pile of money?" a detective asked.

"He never said anything to me...but I could tell he didn't like Philip. They used to work together at the mill...then they both changed jobs."

"That's enough for me," growled the detective, "we have to take a better look at that so-called accident."

The hearing officer was about to postpone the hearing until later in the week when a clerk came in to deliver a note. He read it, looked up and said to Helen "You can have your funeral any time you wish," and excused himself.   Helen was told they would try to get clearance for Philip and Bill to attend Terersa's funeral, if they wanted to attend, but the arrangements were up to her. She was astonished.

"What should we do?" she asked Cynthia and Taylor, who were waiting in the hallway.

"They want me to arrange for Teresa's funeral."

After neither one offered any suggestions, they went to Helen's house where she called a funeral director and the pastor at St. James Church. Teresa was Catholic and had attended Mass at St. James when she was younger. The pastor would conduct the service. She would be buried in the church cemetery. Her body would be cremated.

After the arrangements were made, they sat around the kitchen table having a cup of tea and talking about the customs and traditions of funerals in different parts of the world. Taylor volunteered to read an article on the subject of mourning and burial rites.

All human societies have sought ways to make death acceptable and to provide opportunities for expressing grief and showing respect to the dead person, it began.

In societies where the status of women is low, the mourning and burial rituals are inherently gendered. Rituals are used to exalt the position of the dead man, and his widow is expected to grieve openly and demonstrate the intensity of her feelings in formalized ways. These rituals, prevalent in India as well as among many ethnic groups in Africa, aim at exalting the status of the deceased husband, and they often incorporate the most humiliating, degrading, and life-threatening practices, which effectively punish her for her husband's death.

The widow may be forced to drink the water that the corpse has been washed in; be confined indoors for up to a year;

be prohibited from washing, even if she is menstruating, for several months; be forced to sit naked on a mat and to ritually cry and scream at specific times of the day and night. Many customs cause serious health hazards. The lack of hygiene results in scabies and other skin diseases; those who are not allowed to wash their hands and who are made to eat from dirty, cracked plates may fall victim to gastroenteritis and typhoid. Widows who have to wait to be fed by others become malnourished because the food is poorly prepared.

In both India and Africa, there is much emphasis on dress and lifestyles. Higher-caste Hindu widows must not oil their hair, eat spicy food, or wear bangles, flowers, or the "kumkum" (the red disc on the forehead that is the badge of marriage). Across the cultures, widows are made to look unattractive and unkempt. The ban on spicy foods has its origins in the belief that hot flavors make a widow more lustful. Yet it is widows who are often victims of rape, and many of the vernacular words for "widow" in India and Bangladesh are pejorative and mean "prostitute," "witch," or "sorceress." The terrible stigma and shame of widowhood produces severe depression in millions of women, and sometimes suicide.

The women were listening intently to Taylor read about the treatment of widows in India when the telephone rang, jolting them into reality.

It was a TV station. A reporter wanted to interview her for a story on Teresa's death."I don't think so," she replied. "The investigation is in the hands of the police. "I've said all I'm going to say to the police...you ask them to comment."

"Wait a minute," interrupted Taylor, "What are you guys doing about my father's murder?"

"What is she talking about?" the reporter asked.

A flustered Helen was about to hang up the phone...when she glanced out the front window and saw two TV vans parked in the street...videographers scampering around ready to take pictures of her house...and a well-dressed reporter, phone in hand, waving to be recognized.

"He's the one on the telephone," gasped Helen. "I don't want to talk to him!" She cried out as she slammed the phone down. "We are getting ready to bury my sister...we are in the middle of planning for a funeral...the family is in mourning. Don't they have any respect?" she muttered under her breath.

Mary, Bill's youngest sister, volunteered to go out to the TV crews to tell them "there will be no interview. Period!" She got halfway, yelling for them to go away, when a police car drove up and the officer told them they were blocking traffic.

Two days later--with no interference from TV crews--the pastor of St. James officiated at a Mass for Teresa, concluded the burial of her remains with the prayer "May her soul, and the souls of all the all faithful departed through the mercy of God, rest in peace. Amen."

"Rest in peace Teresa," repeated Helen, who then invited everyone to her home for a bite to eat. A police car took Philip and Bill back to jail, where they were being held as suspects in Teresa's death. Both were fingerprinted and photographed before being locked up.

Among friends consoling Helen over the death of her sister was Mrs. Elizabeth Hanford, a neighbor and elderly matriarch of the Hanford family. The 97-year-old widow had attended more weddings and funerals than she could count, she once told Helen. She had six children before her husband died in World War II, had 17 grandchildren,a couple dozen great grandchildren and has at least three great-great grandchildren.

Elizabeth was living with a grandson who is an eleventh generation direct descendant of the Rev. Thomas Hanford, an English minister who landed in Norwalk, Connecticut in 1he 1600s. Her grandson said she doesn't care too much above wanting to live in a nursing home.

They got to talking about ancestry when Helen reminded her of their search for Teresa. "No one kept any records of her family," said Helen. "How is it that you know so much about your family?"

Elizabeth, who was a little hard of hearing, reacted with a smile. "I have to thank my grandson and my grandson's great grandsons for getting the information," she said. "Mostly ancestors who kept church records of births, marriages and deaths in those early years," she recalled.

"Right now, there are thousands of Hanford's in the country...many of them offspring of widows and widowers who settled in the Western Reserve," she boasted.

"If you are still searching for the Townsend's I'll get my grandson to help you," Elizabeth offered.

"Thank you very much but I think we will find what we were looking for soon," predicted Helen.

The hearings continued for another few days, getting the prosecutor ready for a presentation to the grand jury. There was some hesitation about the charges and the police had not yet located what Philip had done with the family fortune.

In the meantime, Helen had a second thought about getting Elizabeth's grandson David to tell her more about the history of Hanford family. She called to see if the offer was still good and wound up spending the evening visiting with Elizabeth and her grandson.

He was prepared with a genealogical report, picture albums, marriage and death certificates, letters, the "family tree,"and stories describing the hardships experienced by early settlers. "I got a lot of information from the Western Reserve Historical Society, the VA, the National Register and letters to historical libraries in Nowalk and a few other sources, including websites, he confessed.

He showed Helen where he placed in the line of direct descendent from Rev. Thomas Hanford. "My father was a tenth generation Hanford," he pointed out.

He said the first three or four generations settled in the area around Norwalk, Connecticut. "As the families grew, they sought safety from marauding indians and British troops by moving to the New York colony. When word got out about the sale of property in the Western Reserve, and the colonies creation of a free and independent new nation, immigrants arrived by the thousands to build communities and a new life for their families.

"Unfortunately," he added, "the British had other ideas and sent troops to take over the country. Our family lost a lot of good men in the War of 1812. But the wives and widows hung on to help build communities like Cleveland, Ashtabula, Warren, Youngstown, Mansfield. Middlefield and others...

"Also unfortunately," David continued, "the government practically ignored the names of wives and widows in casualty reports, making it very difficult for widows to prove their marriage and thus qualify for military death benefits."

As an example, he pulled out a court file on a case involving the military service of Irus Hanford, a 7th generation direct descendant of Rev.Thomas Hanford. Irus died in 1865 of Typhoid Fever while in the service at Point of Rock, Virginia. His widow and mother of three small children, Nancy A. Dezell, was successful in winning her case.

In another significant court case involving Irus Hanford, his widow Nancy remarried and shared guardianship of her seven-year-old boy Charles with Wesley F. Hill. The case, appealed to the Supreme Court of the State of New York, concerned the stepfather's right to charge for the support of the stepson. He told the court he spent almost six hundred and seventy dollars per year on the boy. Nancy was entitled to receive about seventy-five dollars of her son's pension money until he arrived at the age of sixteen.

"Later, when a large number of Hanfords served in the war between the states, the government made provisions available for all servicemen to provide benefits for widows and young members of their families.

"We have had several close calls that nearly ended the

string of direct descendants David acknowledged. "Irus' first born son, Charles Warren, married Harriet Lamkin in 1881. They had three children, including Arthur George Hanford, my grandfather. Arthur George married Mary Demetri in 1905. Arthur Louis was only nine months old when his father was killed in a railroad accident at Harvard and Broadway in Cleveland.

"There is no explanation of why Mary Hanford, Arthur George's widow, apparently was unable to get railroad death benefits. In any case, she remarried and had three more children. The second husband also died, leaving the family destitute.

"Mary's son, Arthur Louis, helped raise his siblings and married Anastasia in 1929. They had two boys--Arthur Lewis Jr. and Ronald. Ronald, a widower, had three children before he died in 1994. Arthur Jr. and wife Janice, have five married children, a dozen grandchildren and three great grandchildren. I'm one of those grandchildren.

Helen thanked David for taking the time to describe his family's ancestry. "It will be very helpful, I'm sure," she said. Elizabeth, who had been listening to the conversation, was fast asleep.

When she finally got back to home, there were a half-dozen messages on her answering machine. She figured they were from newspaper and TV reporters but was pleasantly surprised to hear from a niece in Arizona.

"I saw this report from Cleveland about aunt Teresa'a death...is it true...was she murdered?" she asked.

Oh my God, Clara," Helen responded. "I can't believe they would broadcast that story. Yes, she's dead but I don't know if she was murdered. We buried her a few days ago. They are holding her son and grandson as suspects...what else did they say on TV?" she asked.

"Well, they mentioned that uncle John was a helicopter pilot in Vietnam, an expert in picking up trapped and wounded soldiers, when he was shot down and killed. They said the widow--aunt Teresa--was given a huge death benefit but her son took the money and abandoned his family. She won custody of the kids...she raised them...and they also abandoned her...and police found her dead body."

"I'll be darned," exclaimed Helen. "I don't know what to believe...I'm going to wait for the trial...if they ever have one."

Another message was from officials at the mill, where her son Howard was killed almost ten years ago.

"We wanted to tell you that workmen cleaning the area where your son was killed have found an old hacksaw that could have been used to tamper with the device," the message began. We have alerted the detective investigating the accident and expect to see him here at any moment."

The device--part of a large air filter system designed to detect dangerous fumes in the mill--had been reinstalled under heavy overhead beams without difficulty. No one had spotted the saw during the original investigation. Whoever used it may have left a fingerprint.

CHAPTER VIII

FINGERPRINTS ID SUSPECTS

There was no way of telling how long the hacksaw had been laying in that pile of rubble but there was speculation one might have been used to cause the accident that killed her son. Still "who could have done such a thing? and why?" Helen asked herself.

She was going to call Cynthia to tell her about the hacksaw, but decided she had other things to do. Instead, she called the detective who had told her about finding Teresa's body. She wanted to know if she could visit her sister's home to see if she could find any reference to their family history.

Their father--Art Donley--had passed away while they were still young, and their widowed mother did everything she could to maintain a family life. Relatives were scarce and scattered around the country. Then there was the problem of finding out how Philip managed to switch his mother's military death benefits to his secret account. Her sister's husband, a marine helicopter pilot, was killed in action in Vietnam.

"Why don't you leave what Philip may have done to government investigators," he advised her. "And as far as visiting that house...I have to warn you..it is no longer an active crime scene but there may be a stench from the dead body."

"I never thought of that," Helen sniffed, who then asked "would it be okay if I just looked around?"

"I suggest you keep notes on anything you find...but go ahead...and good luck." he said.

Recalling how David Hanford, the neighbor who demonstrated how to put together a family history, Helen approached Teresa's home armed with a small briefcase, notebook and camera. The windows were cracked open... apparently to help get rid of the stench.

The door was open and...except for some old furniture... the house was empty. "Somebody came in here and cleaned the place out," she thought. No pictures on the walls...nothing in the cabinets...no kitchen utensils. "I was surprised to find some carpeting on the floors," she wrote in her notebook. She could tell by the dust on the shelves that there must have been a lot of books...or maybe picture albums...and she was going to find out.

"We found some medication, some bedding and some soiled clothes, but that's all," the detective told her. "Sorry," he half-heartily apologized, adding "Maybe her son or grandson may know what happened to all those things...if we get a chance we'll ask them."

It wasn't funny to Helen...Philip and Bill were in jail. She had spent the last few months trying to find her sister. Now, she's gone...and maybe the entire family history with her.

Helen was heading out the door of the police station when it occurred to her that the Western Reserve Historical Society would be the best place to continue her search for family history.

Her neighbor, Dave, told her that the WRHS had data bases and indexes on published materials (books, family histories, pamphlets, microfilm, periodicals, newspapers, etc.,) and unpublished collections (personal papers, organizational records, photographs, etc.). He also told her that the WRHS has a genealogy index, a name search of various genealogical resources including funeral home records, voter registration, cemetery inscriptions, marriage and death notices, Bible records, biographical sketches, and photographs.

Researchers can access and make copies from the collections at the Western Reserve Historical Society Research Center Reading Room. Reference staff can provide copies for researchers unable to schedule a visit. If you want information about the WRHS Research Center location, hours, admission fees, and research fees, contact the reference staff at 216-721-5722, x1509, or via email at reference@wrhs.org.

Another source Helen may have overlooked were church records. She knew that her sister and her husband attended Mass regularly before he left to serve in Vietnam. They were married at a military chapel in Pensacola, Florida, and had one son--Philip. She didn't know his hometown, school, if he was a member of any organizations or how they met in the first place. That could have been in the late 40s or early 50s.

In early colonial days, churches were the center of community activities and it became the custom for ministers or an assigned member of the congregation to keep a journal of births, marriages, deaths...and sometimes seating assignments in the church. If the settlement was under attack, they would find a way to protect the journal. Often, it was the only source of a family's history.

Nowadays, when it is possible for government agencies use computers to collect information on billions of people... researchers no longer have to rely on old journals. But the church would be a good place to start.

In her research, Helen took note that the United States federal government was the first national government to have no official state-endorsed religion. Some states, however, had established religions in some form until the 1930s.

The text of the First Amendment to the country's Constitution states that "Congress shall make no law respecting an establishment of religion, or prohibiting the free exercise thereof; or abridging the freedom of speech, or of the press; or the right of the people peaceably to assemble, and to petition the Government for a redress of grievances." It guarantees the free exercise of religion while also preventing the government from establishing a state religion.

Kip Sperry, a professor of church history at Case Western Reserve University when he wrote an article on religion and ethnicity in the Western Reserve, tells how northeastern Ohio attracted diverse religious and ethnic groups during the first half of the nineteenth century. Following are excerpts from his article:

Most of the earliest settlers in the Western Reserve arrived from the New England states, New York, and other states during the late eighteenth century, and the influx continued throughout the nineteenth century. Settlers immigrated to this region for a variety of economic reasons, including opportunities in farming, industry, and factories; work on the railroads and canals; and desire for better land. In addition, a combination of personal considerations influenced the migration: religious, military, and political concerns; the desire to settle in an area with other immigrants from the old country or family members; to improve social conditions; and to search for a new life. The Reserve's favorable weather also attracted a number of immigrants, especially those from the New England states. During the years 1816 and 1817, New Englanders endured particularly cold winters, and many farmers lost their crops. It is not surprising that a mass migration to northeastern Ohio occurred as New Englanders sought rich farmland elsewhere. After arriving in northeastern Ohio, settlers concentrated on farming their land, working at an occupation, and getting used to their new environment.

An influx of New England emigrants arrived in the Western Reserve after the War of 1812. Some followed ministers or other religious leaders. The townships were mostly patterned after New England towns, while some carried the same or similar names. A number of townships included a central green containing a Congregational meetinghouse (or other church), a town hall, and the local schoolhouse. Later, large industrial centers in Cleveland, such as iron and steel factories, provided jobs for thousands of migrants. Akron also had manufacturing and rubber plants that attracted workers with diverse ethnic backgrounds....

Northeastern Ohio also drew thousands of European immigrants from the mid- to late nineteenth century and into the twentieth century. Immigrants from European countries traveled to Cleveland and northeastern Ohio for a number of reasons—economic and religious considerations, epidemics in the old country, political persecution, and to avoid being drafted into the military, among other concerns. "Between 1860 and 1930 a majority of the people who came to Cleveland and other large Great Lakes cities in the United States—Buffalo, Detroit, Chicago, Milwaukee—came from Central, Southern and Eastern Europe. Throughout those years, Cleveland was one of the most 'European' of all American cities....."

Biographies, census records after 1850, church records, early land records, and local histories (such as county histories) are useful in identifying the origins of immigrants to Ohio counties....

Pioneers who settled in northeastern Ohio engaged in a variety of religious practices. Rural settlers were not often active in formal religion, likely because of the distance between farms and communities with churches, but for the most part they were good Christians. The majority of white settlers to the Western Reserve in the early nineteenth century were New England Yankees—primarily arriving from Connecticut and Massachusetts. These Protestants brought with them their Congregational and Presbyterian beliefs....

Initially, settlers who wished to hold religious services met in cabins, homes, or barns, and sometimes in the town meetinghouse or courthouse. Later, resident pastors were found, and log meeting houses and permanent church buildings were erected. While some settlers were not interested in theology and chose not to be associated with any religious organization, believer and nonbeliever alike were served by traveling missionaries, itinerant pastors, circuit preachers, and circuit riders. Most of these clergymen were Baptist, Congregationalist, Methodist, or Presbyterian....

Foreign immigrants to the Western Reserve tended to gather in homogeneous communities with others who shared their language, customs, and traditions. To assist immigrants, churches established charities, social groups, fraternal organizations, hospitals, missionary societies, religious orders, schools, and similar institutions for its members. The Congregationalist influence brought in by New Englanders, especially immigrants from Connecticut in the late eighteenth and early nineteenth centuries, later expanded to include Protestant, Roman Catholic, Jewish, and other religious organizations. Religious diversity and pluralism in the Western Reserve was evident after the Civil War and into the early twentieth century as churches and synagogues cooperated with one another....

Roman Catholic settlements could be found in the Western Reserve beginning in the early nineteenth century. The Catholic Church was particularly strong in larger industrial cities, including Akron, Cleveland, and Youngstown. The Diocese of Cleveland (also known as the Cleveland Catholic Diocese) was organized in 1847. Many nineteenth-century European immigrants to the Reserve were members of the Roman Catholic Church—Germans, Irish, Italians, and central Europeans. Irish Catholics were one of the largest religious groups in the greater Cleveland area. Roman Catholics migrated to northeastern Ohio to work on the Ohio and Erie Canal or to work in Cleveland's industries. Roman Catholics established parishes, parochial schools, hospitals, and other institutions. The Roman Catholic Church today forms one of the largest religious bodies in Ohio. Roman Catholic Church records may be found in individual churches and in diocesan offices and archives. Roman Catholic baptismal records, marriage record books, newspapers, and other records are also housed at the Immigration History Research Center in Minneapolis, Minnesota, and the Western Reserve Historical Society in Cleveland....

Among other religious groups described in Professor Sperry's article were the Amish, who settled in Holmes and Geauga Counties in the 1880s; Baptists, one of the largest religious groups in Ohio who are important to the African-American community; Congregationalists, a religion in which each congregation is autonomous and self-governing; Disciples of Christ, a Protestant movement established in the Western Reserve in the 1820s; Episcopalians, which played a major role in the Cleveland Underground Railroad, was first established in Warren, Ohio in 1813; Jews, who settled in Cleveland and Akron rather than rural farming communities; Lutherans, established in early Cleveland by German immigrants; Mennonites; Methodists; Latter-day Saints; Presbyterians; Shakers; United Church of Christ; Unitarians; Universalists, and numerous other religious organizations.

What about those people who have no religion?

According to a 2002 survey by the Pew Research Center, nearly 6 in 10 Americans said that religion plays an important role in their lives, compared to 33% in Great Britain, 27% in Italy, 21% in Germany, 12% in Japan, and 11% in France. The survey report stated that the results showed America having a greater similarity to developing nations (where higher percentages say that religion plays an important role) than to other wealthy nations, where religion plays a minor role.

In 1963, 90% of U.S. adults claimed to be Christian while

only 2% professed no religious identity. In 2014, close to 70% identify as Christian while close to 23% claim no religious identity.

It wasn't exactly what her neighbor David had in mind, but Helen's next thought was to see the pastor at St. James to see if he could head her in the right direction. She called to find out the pastor was at a Knights of Columbus meeting, but left a message asking him if there was any chance his church might have any record of John Townsend.

The next day, they had a very pleasant conversation about her sister's family and how being a widow made things a little more stressful, especially when it came to Teresa's son and grandson. The priest assured her he would look up any records his church might have and get back to her as soon as he can.

The police and federal investigators were not nearly as interested as Helen about John Townsend's ancestry but they were trying to find out what happened to the nearly half-million dollars taken from the family bank account. Some thought the two mysteries were bound together in one grand theft (another unintended pun).

Helen's research resulted in thousands of "Townsend" names from all over the world, but none matched his age, place of birth, and other important data to make a positive identification. There was one possibility.

David, Helen's neighbor, once recently told her the story about how his grandfather had two names. His grandfather was only nine months old when his father, George Hanford, was killed in a railroad accident in 1906. His mother remarried a few years later to William Green and they had three more children. His grandfather, so young at the time, lived as a member of the Green family, even though he was a "Hanford." After his stepfather died, he was raised by his widowed mother as a "Green." In school, he used "Green" as his last name. In the Conservation Corps he used "Green" as his last name. He went out west for a short time and came back to Cleveland using his real name..."Hanford."

According to the family, all they knew about the stepfather was that he was called a "commodore," because he practically lived on a boat in Sandusky, Ohio. His great grandmother, a widow again with four children, was destitute. She got help from the Salvation Army and operated a candy store until the children were old enough to marry...three of them Green, and one Hanford. Their mother died in a fire in 1937.

Is it possible that John Townsend had a similar past? Did his father have a different name--a name he and his family used to hide that stash of money?

Helen recalled that detectives investigating her sister's death located Philip and his son Bill by tracing a real estate transaction in West Virginia to a man from Cleveland who called himself Pat Tordaloni. They apparently did not check out any connection between the Townsend and Tortaloni names. They should have.

Pat Tordaloni (John Townsend) was born in 1927 in a small mining town in West Virginia. His father, Angelo Tordaloni, was killed in a mining accident when he was very young. Teresa and Angelo had one son, Philip, born in 1946. Philip kept his father's name (birth certificates, school records, etc.) until his mother remarried to John Townsend in 1952. After Townsend's death in Vietnam, Philip transferred the family fortune to a Tordaloni account with the hope that nobody but he would have access to the money.

Philip would have been desperate to know if anyone had learned of his scheme to take government benefit money from his mother, and his wife and children. He knew that Howard Beck, Helen's married son, had overheard him one day talking on the telephone about his plan to leave and buy property in another state.

He was told he could be guilty of fraud that could be very easily traced, and could expect to be subject to IRS review. In either case, he was advised to get a lawyer and be ready to go to jail.

As previously noted, Philip had abandoned his aged and ill mother, changed their names to Tordaloni, and left her and his wife and three children to live on his mother's VA Death Pension benefits. A short time later, Philip's wife also disappeared, leaving her mother-in-law to take care of the children.

The police were examining that hacksaw to see if there were any fingerprints. Philips wife, hoping for some reward money, told them where her husband and son were hiding. The police found them and took them into custody.

Now she knew why Bill was telling everyone his grandmother did not want any visitors. And it was time to tell Taylor and Cynthia what she had learned.

Cynthia was not home but Helen had a key to the side door. Instead of waiting for them to come home, she started looking for some paper to write a note. Her daughter-in-law and granddaughter were using a home computer for almost everything, including finances and research on family ancestry. It was tempting to take a look but she knew it would be an invasion of privacy and not worth the risks if caught. One unopened letter on the desk caught her eye. It was addressed to Cynthia from...Pat Tordaloni!! and postmarked a month ago from Huntington, W.Va.

"What's this all about?" she wondered..and began shifting between some wild thoughts.

She still had the envelope in her hands when the front door popped open and her granddaughter came hopping in. She ran straight to Helen, gave her a big hug and went back to help her mother with the groceries.

"Hi mom...what brings you here in the middle of a sunny afternoon?" Cynthia squealed, as she unloaded on the sink and gave her mother-in-law a peck on the cheek.

"Well, it seems the police have figured out how Philip has managed to squirrel away his mother's money and I thought you might like to know," Helen gushed. "What's new with you guys?" she asked.

"I got this letter from a Pat Tordaloni," Cynthia exclaimed as she picked it up to show Helen, "and I'm not sure what to do with it."

"I know the detective that's working on this case," Helen responded, "lets give him a call to see what he wants you to do."

After a few minutes, as the operator paged the detective, he finally answered and signaled for an associate to listen in on the conversation.

"Sir," Cynthia began, "I have an envelope sent to me by a Pat Tordaloni. In it is a check for five hundred dollars and a card expressing sympathy over Howard's accident. What do you want me to do with it?"

"I'll send an" officer to pick it up," he answered after confirming Cynthia's address and phone number...don't handle it any more than you have to...put it in a plastic bag, if you have one."

A few hours later, the detective called Cynthia to tell her there were three distinct fingerprints identified on the letter. One was hers, another was Helen's and the third...Bill Townsend... or "whatever he calls himself."

"Let me get this straight," Cynthia inquired, "Why would Bill Townsend send me 500 dollars?"

"That's something you may have to answer under oath in court," the detective calmly responded, "and he may have to explain where he got the money."

After Cynthia hung up the phone, the three of them-- including Helen and Taylor--sat in the living room to discuss the latest revelation.

"I picked it up to see who sent it...that's all," reported Helen.

"Now I'm asking the same question...why would Bill Townsend send you money?"

They were discussing the possible reasons why Bill sent the money when a police car drove up and the detective who Cynthia had just called climbed out, and walked slowly to her door. Taylor ushered him into the living room.

Cynthia went to get the bag with the letter.

"I'll take that...but I have some other news pertaining to your husband's accident," he uttered. "We found some fingerprints on that rusty hacksaw found near the area where he was knocked from a ladder. They are a match to Bill Townsend's prints."

"Oh my God!" gushed Helen, tears flowing and a hand grasping her jaw. "Does that mean Bill was the one who caused my son's death? What was he doing there? He didn't work at the mill...how could he?"

"Nothing is proven yet," insisted the detective, "but we have to consider everything when it comes to murder...I hope you understand."

Cynthia collapsed into a chair, unable to speak. Could she be implicated in some way to her husband's death? Taylor, too, wondered if Cynthia's original opposition to her grandmother's search for Townsend ancestry may have been an attempt to cover up Bill's involvement in the crime.

Helen wanted to go home.

CHAPTER IX

THE FOREMOTHERS

While investigators were trying to figure out who to charge in the deaths of Teresa Townsend and Howard Beck, there was a third person missing and unaccounted for. She was Philip's wife, a fashion model that had seen better days, now pushing her sixties.

Philip and Margaret, married in 1955, had three children-- Bill, Mary and Anita. They lived with Philip's mother. Margaret had a part-time job in a women's clothing store and loved outdoor sports, especially golf. Philip preferred hunting, fishing and gambling.

The two of them got along all right but argued incessantly about his elderly mother's care and his drinking binges. He expected her to spend her free time tending to his mother's every wish and taking care of their three young children. He had a habit of echoing his mother's complaints. She couldn't take it anymore, so she left, abandoning her children.

"That was in the late 90s," said Mary, the oldest of the two girls. She and Anita left a few years later, staying with relatives... Bill stayed home, alledgedly to take care of his grandmother.

Complicating the estrangement was Philip's handling of the huge VA Death Benefit awarded to Teresa after her husband's death in Vietnam. Whether it was legal or not, it didn't stop him from stashing the money in a foreign bank under a different name, with full control of the account.

"He was able to get away with that for quite a while... until he decided to buy some property in West Virginia...and Howard Beck heard him talk about it," said one of the federal agents investigating fraud.

According to a government explanation, you commit benefit fraud by either:

- Intentionally not reporting a change in your circumstances
- Being dishonest in order to get benefits

If you are suspected of fraud, you'll be contacted by the Department for Work and Pensions, HM Revenue and Customs, the Service and Personnel and Veteran Agency or your local authority. You may be visited by Fraud Investigation Officers (FIO's) or asked to attend an interview to talk about your claim. Your benefit may be stopped while you are investigated. You'll get a letter telling you about this if it happens. FIOs will gather facts about your case and decide whether to take further action.

If there's evidence you've committed fraud, you'll be told to pay back the overpaid money. One or more of the following may also happen:

- You may be taken to court or asked to pay a penalty
- Your benefits may be reduced or stopped

Your benefits can be reduced or stopped for up to three years if you're convicted of benefit fraud. The amount of time they're stopped for depends on how many times you've committed fraud.

Only certain benefits can be reduced or stopped. These are called 'sanctionable benefits'. But, if you commit fraud on a benefit that can't be reduced or stopped, your other benefits can be reduced instead.

Everyone in the Beck and Townsend families got one of those letters alerting them to the possibility of getting a visit from a Fraud Investigation Officer...he visited, asked a few questions, but, until now, no one has been notified about any action.

The police, meanwhile, have been gathering evidence on two deaths and a missing mother. No charges had yet been filed.

There wasn't much Cynthia or anyone else could do, except perhaps pray for a favorable solution.

The history of women in Cleveland and the Western Reserve is documented through over 300 manuscripts and photograph collections that illustrate the contributions of women in the early settlement of the Western Reserve, the roles they played in the development of the region, and their influences on public life, changes in women's lives as they started their own businesses, were elected to public office, joined professions, and became active in the labor movement. The collections also shed light on changes in home life, marriage, and gender roles in the Western Reserve.

The collections document the lives of professional women, workers, and volunteers in fields as diverse as the law, education, the military, education, philanthropy, religion, and social work. The collections show the contributions of female judges, attorneys, teachers, physicians, nurses, social workers, and homemakers in the Civil Rights Movement, and the Equal Rights Movement.

Helen also found an interesting source of information for researchers titled: *Memorial to the Pioneer Women of the Western Reserve*. The Memorial, edited by Mrs. Gertrude Van Renselaer Wickham, is said to be nearly a thousand pages "written about women, by women" and dates back to the 1800s. The three volume set of books. completed in 1924, is especially helpful because it provides both maiden and married surnames for women, as well as personal information that is not available anywhere else. It was assembled by Mrs. Wickham after her appointment as historian by the Cleveland Centennial Commission in 1895. It was fitting, one reviewer observed, that "time had come in which to treat—not of the services, as usual, or our forefathers—but, if the term be admissible, of our foremothers."

Other statistics about widows cleaned from various publications, including *Widows Hope*, were:

According to the U.S. Census Bureau **800,000 people are widowed** each year in the United States. "Nearly **700,000 women lose their husbands** each year and will be widows for an average of 14 years" - *U.S. Bureau of the Census (1999)*

There are **13.6 million** widows in the United States. Over 11 million of the widowed, in the US, are women. (American Association of Retired Persons 2001) UNITED NATIONS (AP) 6/23/2010 —

At least 245 million women around the world have been widowed and more than **115 million of them live in devastating poverty,** according to a study launched by Cherie Blair, wife of the former British prime minister. According to the report, the countries with the highest number of widows in 2010 were China with 43 million, India with 42.4 million, the United States with 13.6 million, Indonesia with 9.4 million, Japan with 7.4 million, Russia with 7.1 million, Brazil with 5.6 million, Germany with 5.1 million, and Bangladesh and Vietnam with about 4.7 million each.

Death of a spouse is ranked as the #1 Stressor: Holmes and Rahe Stress Scale. Losing a spouse is ranked number one on the stress index scale; making this one of life's most devastating events. The stress chart assigns a numerical point value to each life stressor. Death of a spouse scores 100 points. Oftentimes there is a snowball effect of stressors that occur as a result of the loss. **Scores of 300+** indicate a strong risk of illness.

With knowledge and proper care, we can prevent or lesson this statistic: **60%** of those who lose a spouse or significant other will **experience a serious illness** in the 12 months following that loss. Those widowed have reported illnesses like cancer, pancreas' shutting down, shingles....Widows and the friends and family that love them need to be aware of the snowball effect of such a staggering loss. We encourage you to take care of yourself!

Sleep can be severely impacted with the loss of a spouse. Disrupted sleep makes it harder to handle our grief, our lives, and even the day-to-day duties of making the bed or paying the bills. And it may also affect our health. Read More: How to Cope with Grief and Learn to Sleep Alone

Widowhood increases survivors' risk of dying. According to the American Public Health Journal: This longitudinal study of 373 189 elderly American couples shows that the effect of widowhood on mortality varies substantially by the causes of death of both spouses. We found these results for husbands and wives, even after adjusting for a wide range of potentially confounding factors, including the health of both spouses. **Widowhood** increases survivors' risk of dying from almost all causes, including cancer, but it increases the risk for some causes more than for others. The converse also holds: widowhood increases survivors' all-cause mortality in response to almost all causes of death of the predecedent spouse, but the actual cause of death of the predecedent spouse makes a difference. The death of a spouse, for whatever reason, is a significant threat to health and poses a substantial risk of death by whatever cause.

On average **75% of the survivor's support base is lost** following the loss of a spouse or significant other; this includes loss of support from family and friends. There are a multitude of reasons for losing friends and family including; loss of couples friends. Those widowed can isolate, we can be sad and unpleasant to be around. Family members are grieving and they go through the unpleasant stages of grief. We take on more responsibility (taking care of a house and/or children). Life changes in huge ways and we need to build new friendships and support systems.

85 percent of consumers agree that most people need life insurance, yet just **62 percent** say they have it. *Source: LIMRA's Life Insurance Barometer Study 2013*

44 percent of U.S. households had individual life insurance as of 2010 — a 50-year low. In 1960, **72 percent** of Americans owned individual life insurance. In 1992, **55 percent** owned it. *Source: LIMRA's Trends in Life Insurance Ownership study*

40 percent of Americans who have life insurance coverage don't think they have enough. *Source: Genworth LifeJacket Study 2011*

70 percent of U.S. households with children under 18 would have trouble meeting everyday living expenses within a few months if a primary wage earner were to die today. **4 in 10** households with children under 18 say they would immediately have trouble meeting everyday living expenses.

People who feel consistently lonely have a **14% higher risk** of premature death than those who don't, a new study shows.

The impact of loneliness on early death is almost as strong as being poor, which increased the chances of dying early by 19% the research found. "Loneliness is a risk factor for early death beyond what can be explained by poor health behaviors," says psychologist John Cacioppo, Director of the Center for Cognitive and Social Neuroscience at the University of Chicago. *Source: USA Today*

Can a person really die of a broken heart? Found in *Star Tribune Variety* Section E, Wednesday, June 4, 2014. *By Allie Shah*

"It's very real," said Dr. Scott Sharkey, a cardiologist with the Minneapolis Heart Institute at Abbott Northwestern Hospital. Doctors even have a not-so-subtle name for it: broken heart syndrome. "Any cardiologist in town will tell you that they've seen several cases of this," Sharkey said. He studies the medical condition, which is triggered by sudden, major stress. The symptoms are similar to a heart attack: shortness of breath, chest pains, an accelerated heartbeat. For senior citizens, this type of sudden heart injury can be especially dangerous when combined with pre-existing conditions and their age.

Researchers at the University of Glasgow conducted a large study of more than 4,000 married couples, ages 45 to 64, and found that widows and widowers had a 30 percent elevated risk of death in the first 6 months after their spouses had died.

One bereaved in five is likely to develop a psychiatric disorder… the highest rate are found in boys. *Journal of Child Psychology, Oct. 2000*

In a survey of 300 incarcerated teens, 96% indicated that someone significant in their lives had died. *Columbia University*

85% of all prisoners on death row experienced the death of a parent during their childhood. *Virginia Simpson PHD, The Mourning Star Center, CA*

Between 5% and 7.5% of all children are actively grieving. *US Census Bureau*

"Almost half the women over 65 years of age in the United States are widows. About 7 in 10 of these women live alone." (U.S. Census, 2000) In recent years the average American woman's expected lifespan has increased to eighty or more. However, the societal systems in place for caring for the elderly have not changed at the same rapid pace leaving many **widows** in poverty.

One Social Security Administration report shows that **"for the past thirty or more years the rate of poverty among elderly widows is consistently three to four times higher than elderly married women."** *(SSA, 2005)*

In societies where the husband is the sole provider, his death can leave his family destitute. The tendency for women generally to outlive men can compound this, since men in many societies marry women younger than themselves. In some patriarchal societies, widows may maintain economic independence. A woman would carry on her spouse's business and be accorded certain rights, such as entering guilds. More recently, widows of political figures have been among the first women elected to high office in many countries, such as Corazón Aquino or Isabel Martínez de Perón.

In 19th-century Britain, widows had greater opportunity for social mobility than in many other societies. Along with the ability to ascend socio-economically, widows—who were "presumably celibate"—were much more able (and likely) to challenge conventional sexual behaviour than married women in their society.

In some parts of Europe, including Russia, Czechoslovakia,

Greece, Italy and Spain, widows used to wear black for the rest of their lives to signify their mourning, a practice that has since died out. Many immigrants from these cultures to the United States as recently as the 1970s have loosened this strict standard of dress to only two years of black garments. However, Orthodox Christian immigrants may wear lifelong black in the United States to signify their widowhood and devotion to their deceased husband.

In other cultures, however, widowhood customs are stricter. Often, women are required to remarry within the family of their late husband after a period of mourning. With the rise of HIV/AIDS levels infection across the globe, rituals to which women are subjected in order to be "cleansed" or accepted into her new husband's home make her susceptible to the psychological adversities that may be involved as well as imposing health risks.

It is often necessary for a woman to comply with the social customs of her area because her fiscal stature depends on it, but this custom is also often abused by others as a way to keep money within the patriarchal family. It is also uncommon for widows to challenge their treatment because they are often "unaware of their rights under the modern law...because of their low status, and lack of education or legal representation."

As of 2004, women in United States who were "widowed at younger ages are at greatest risk for economic hardship." Similarly, married women who are in a financially unstable household are more likely to become widows "because of the strong relationship between mortality [of the male head] and wealth [of the household]."

In underdeveloped and developing areas of the world, conditions for widows continue to be much more severe. However, the United Nations Convention on the Elimination of All Forms of Discrimination against Women ("now ratified by 135 countries"), while slow, is working on proposals which will make certain types of discrimination and treatment of widows (such as violence and withholding property rights) illegal in the countries that have joined CEDAW.

During the investigation of Howard Beck and Teresa Townsend deaths, the police were finally able to discover a strong suspect with a solid motive in the case:

It was discovered that Philip Townsend -shortly after his father's death in Vietnam--had emptied his father's bank account...falsified a death notice...left his children with a widowed and pennyless mother....changed his identity...and disappeared. A nationwide search had been unable to locate him...until recently...when he was charged with theft...and brought in for trial.

While everyone's attention was on the Townsend case... it was suspected...that Taylor's father, Howard Beck, was not killed in an industrial accident...but was murdered when he learned Phillip's new identity and threatened to reveal where he was hiding.

Faulty equipment was blamed but it was no accident...it had been arranged to make it look like an accident.....worse yet...Taylor's widowed mother, Cynthia, suspected what Philip had done but kept it a secret. Philip's greedy wife, Margaret, saw an opportunity to get rich.

Teresa had married John Townsend in 1952 after her first husband--Angelo Tordaloni--died from natural causes. Teresa and John had one son--Philip--who was born in 1955. John was killed in action in Vietnam in 1973. Teresa was awarded a $100,000 military death benefit, and a big life insurance payment, saving Philip the trouble of having to work for a living.

Philip met and married Margaret in 1995. They had three children before Philip got restless, did a lot of gambling and drinking, then left his wife and family to take care of his bedridden mother. Margaret was not happy and was looking for a way to latch on to that family fortune.

She knew that Philip had worked with Howard at the steel mill for a short time...maybe she could arrange for Philip to be charged with a crime and get access to the family bank account. She had a bar buddy who was willing to do "almost anything" for a few bucks.

"It has to look like it was a deliberate attempt by Philip and his son to prevent Howard from telling the police where they were hiding," Margaret's hired killer later testified. He also explained how he managed to get Bill's fingerprint on the hacksaw and wore gloves when he dumped it on the pile of rubble.

There was one more thing: Margaret knew Cynthia was suing the company that installed the device. She sent her the $500 check, hoping police would suspect that Cynthia was involved in her husband's death. Margaret paid her accomplice $1,000. He pled guilty and confessed to attempted murder.

In a summation to the jury, the prosecutor outlined his case:

"There are two suspicious deaths," he began, "Howard Beck and Teresa Townsend."

> Howard killed in industrial accident (tampered bolts) lawsuit paid
> Teresa, bedridden widow of Vietnam vet, left alone to die
> Bill joins Phillip in seclusion (name changed from Townsend to Tordaloni)

Suspects ....Philip (abandoned family, took over father's death benefit)
> Bill (solitary fingerprint on saw, access to father's money)
> Margaret, Philip's wife (mother of three...Bill & 2 daughters)
> Cynthia, Howard's widow

Evidence ....Hacksaw with Bill's fingerprint....no other prints found

Severed bolts on device that fell on Howard

Bill's efforts to block Teresa visitors

Name change by Philip, cabin in W.Va.

Envelope with check for $500, with fingerprints

Facts: Philip would have been 18 when his father was killed in Vietnam in 1973

It was not clear if he was eligible for military death benefits at that time

Philip's father had large life insurance policy when killed he was 40 years old when he married Margaret in 1995

His wife (Margaret) left him in 2000 he was 47 when he abandoned his mother, wife and 3 children in 2002

He bought a cabin at a lake resort - changed name to

Tordaloni His mother (Teresa) raised his children--Bill, Mary and Anita He is 62 and in jail, on trial... with his son Bill

Fact: Margaret lived out of state on unknown income

Used Townsend name jn semi-seclusion

She leaves Philip, abandons children

No record of her contact with Philip or son Bill

Accomplice's confession

Fact: Bill, born in 1996, stayed with his grandmother

He had a part-time job repairing lawn mowers

He never finished high school and had a low IQ

His grandmother was already dead when he left

He was afraid to tell anyone where he was going

Fact: Howard died while inspecting a piece of equipment

He was on a high ladder when the device fell on him

Inspectors found bolts holding the device had been weakened

His widow won a lawsuit, claiming unsafe installation

He and his wife, Cynthia, knew where Philip was hiding

Workers found hacksaw with Bill's fingerprint

Fact: Helen finds envelope addressed to Cynthia from Tordaloni

Envelop contains check for $500

Fingerprints on envelop meant to misdirect case

After two days of testimony, exhibits, presentations and cross examinations, the jury was given a number of charges to consider...and instructed to ask questions if they did not understand. What still remained were potential charges of fraud by the Field Investigating Officer.

Philip and his family were waiting for the other shoe to drop.

CHAPTER X

SOMETHING TO CELEBRATE

Everyone was in a somber mood--milling around the court house, barely talking to one another--as they waited for the jury to decide. Reporters kept looking at their watches, hoping to get something before the next deadline. Some TV guys kept their equipment within reach...even when they went to the men's room. Two attractive, blonde TV interviewers kept busy fussing with their hair.

Helen, Taylor, and Cynthia sat near the telephone in Cynthia's living room. The minutes turned to hours and the hours turned to days as they waited for some word from the court house.

"Maybe they can't decide," Taylor said, breaking the silence. "Don't they have to be unanimous when it comes to finding someone guilty? And what if they can't all agree on anything? What do they do?

Later, at about 2:30 in the afternoon, they got a call telling them the jury had made a decision. They would soon find out what "they" can do. Cynthia needed to get over there right away.

The foreman, a portly 50-ish gentleman in a business suit, rose to his feet, buttoned his coat, stiffened his lips, and informed the judge that the panel was "split down the middle."

There was a question of whether Howard's death was caused by an accident and If Teresa died from natural causes.

If the jurors cannot agree on a verdict, a hung jury results, leading to a mistrial. The case is not decided, and it may be tried again at a later date before a new jury. Or the plaintiff or government may decide not to pursue the case further and there will be no subsequent trial.

Before declaring a mistrial in the deaths of Howard Beck and Teresa Townsend, the judge cautioned the defendants that the government was still investigating a suspicion of fraud in the disposition of military death benefits. It would be up to the prosecutor to seek a new trial on charges stemming from the attempt to arrange Howard's death.

The media was having a field day, going over testimony and guessing why a jury would let someone get away with murder. Helen and her daughter-in-law Cynthia felt the same way but were relieved because the trial was over and Helen's sister was at peace.

Their experience as widows in the Western Reserve my not have been as arduous as their predecessors who faced extreme hardship establishing a home in the wilderness, lost their husbands in battles for independence, or the war between the states,

"At least we have our rights as citizens, a home and benefits to supplement our meager Social Security benefits, and people who care about us," declared Cynthia,"but we still have a long way to go. News of the trial spurred a number of groups to comment on the status of widows in the U.S. and around the world.

Helen recorded some of the comments to pass on to her granddaughter, who was in her senior year in high school. Their search for John and Teresa Townsend was over but they wanted to share what they had learned.

One Social Security Administration report shows that "For the past thirty or more years the rate of poverty among elderly widows is consistently three to four times higher than elderly married women."

"While the potential of women is recognized at the international level," said World Health Organization director-general Margaret Chan, "This potential will not be realized until conditions improve – often dramatically – in countries and communities. Too many complex factors, often rooted in social and cultural norms, continue to hinder the ability of women and girls to achieve their potential and benefit from social advances."

Literacy is one of the best indicators of women's status in their countries. Cheryl Hotchkiss of Amnesty International Canada, says building schools alone doesn't solve the problem of equal education.

"There's a huge range of barriers women face to getting an education," she says. "It may be free and available, but parents won't send their daughters out to school if they can be kidnapped and raped."

Health is another key indicator, including the care of pregnant women, who are sometimes forced into disastrous early marriage and childbearing, as well as infection with HIV/AIDS. But again, statistics fail to show the whole, complex story.

"On a rural lake in Zambia, I met a woman who had not told her husband she was HIV-positive," says David Morley, CEO of Save the Children Canada. "She was already living on the edge because she had no children. If she told him, she would be kicked off the island and sent alone to the mainland. She felt she had no choice, because she had no power at all."

Putting power in women's hands is the biggest challenge for improving their lives in every country, advocates agree. Whether in the poorest countries of Africa, or the most repressive of the Middle East or Asia, lack of control over their own destinies blights women's lives from early childhood.

A number of women's groups also commented on the need

to organize efforts to improve the status of women, especially widows.

When widows "band together," organize themselves, make their voices heard, and are represented on decision-making bodies locally, nationally, regionally, and internationally, change will occur. Progress will not be made until widows themselves are the agents of change. Widows' associations must be encouraged and "empowered" to undertake studies profiling their situation and needs.

Widows must be involved in the design of projects and programs and instrumental in monitoring the implementation and effectiveness of new reform legislation to give them property, land, and inheritance rights; protect them from violence; and give them opportunities for training and employment.

Widows at last have an international advocacy organization. In 1996, following a workshop at the Beijing Fourth World Women's Conference, Empowering Widows in Development (EWD) was established. This nongovernmental international organization has ECOSOC consultative status with the United Nations and is a charity registered in the United Kingdom and the United States.

EWD is an umbrella group for more than fifty grass-roots organizations of widows in South Asia, Africa, Eastern Europe, and East Asia and its membership is constantly growing. EWD is focusing on the plight of millions of widows in Afghanistan— Afghan widows in refugee camps. An offshoot of EWD, Widows For Peace and Reconstruction, was set up in August, 2001 to represent the special needs of war widows and to ensure that their voices are heard in post-conflict peace building.

In February 2001 EWD held its first international conference, "Widows Without Rights," in London; participants, widows' groups, and their lawyers came from some fifteen different countries. EWD represents widows at UN meetings, such as the UN Commission on the Status of Women, and is a consultant to various UN agencies on issues of widowhood. At last, widows are becoming visible, and their groups, both grass roots and national, are beginning to have some influence within their countries.

However, much more work is needed to build up the capacity of widows' groups and to educate the United Nations, civil society, governments, and institutions, including the judiciary and the legal profession, on the importance of protecting the human rights of widows and their children in all countries, whether they are at peace or in conflict.

There are a number of organizations right here in Ohio that offer assistance to women who have lost loved ones...here's a couple of them:

WESTERN RESERVE GRIEF SERVICES

Widows who are looking for help may want to check out one of many bereavement support groups offered by Western Reserve Grief Services. Following is a partial list of support groups open to anyone, unless otherwise noted, who has had a loved one die. The groups are subject to change. Registration may be required. If interested, call the number provided to verify time and location.

Restoring Hope: When a Loved One Dies From an Overdose
Ashtabula Office--Susan Hamme 440-596-3582
Center for Inner Peace--Cuyahoga Falls--Mary Murphy 216-763-6442

The LCADA Way--Avon Lake--Judy Beckman 440-414-1731
Grief:
    WR Lakeshsore Campus - Karen Kincaid 216-486-6973
    The Robertson Relief Center--JoDee Coulter 330-662-5240

Hope & Healing:
> Lakeshore Campus - April Ratcliffe - 216-383-3782
> The Robertson Bereavement Center- Theresa Suing 330-241-6282
> Mentor Office - Lisa Florjancic - 440-853-5365

Parent Loss
> West Campus - Judy Beckman - 440-4141731

Parents Together
> Warrensville Heights Ohio - Vicki Jackson 216-763-6441

Hopeful Hearts
> Holy Spirit Parish Center, Avon Lake- Chemarra Bryant 440-414-1737

Adult Support Groups
Circle of Hope
> Ashtabula County Medical Center - Susan Hamme 440-596-3582
> Lakeshore Campus - Tensie Holland 216-383-3741
> Robertson Bereavement Center - Theresa Suing 330-241-6282
> Mentor Office - Lisa Florjancic 440-853-5365
> Warrensville Office- Vicki Jackson 216-763-6441
> West Campus - Judy Beckman 440-414-1731

Cornerstone Of Hope

5905 Brecksville Rd, Independence, OH 44131 (216) 524-4673 General Info * Cornerstone of Hope is a Non-Profit Bereavement Center Designed to Offer Affordable Grief Support to the Entire Family * Guided by Christian Values of Compassion and Service, We Welcome and Serve All Who Seek Support and Healing Spoken Languages: English / Spanish Upon Request.

Widowed Women Who Achieved Greatness

While examining the articles about how some countries treat their widows, Helen, Cynthia and Taylor enjoyed reading articles about notable women in American history. When suffering from the loss of a loved one, the grief can seem so insurmountable that it feels like there's no way around it or through it. Especially acute can be the loss of a spouse—how to go on without the person you partnered with for life? Following is a selection of articles and books written about American women that have achieved greatness after the loss of their husbands.

1. **Mary Todd Lincoln: Conquered Stigma of Mental Illness**. Did she suffer from mental illness, post-traumatic stress disorder from multiple deaths in her family or did she merely exhibit strong emotions? Perhaps more fascinating than her life in the White House is what she did after Abraham Lincoln was assassinated: Consumed by grief in the wake of her husband's death, Lincoln was the first U.S. president's widow to secure a lifelong pension, a measure of independence rare for women in her era. She maintained correspondence with friends including Queen Victoria, who had become a widow four years before Lincoln.

2. **Coretta Scott King: Major Strides for Civil Rights.** More than 100 years after Lincoln's death, another champion of equality was assassinated, and his wife would carry on his legacy for decades. Coretta Scott King knew what she was getting into when she married Martin Luther King Jr. a life devoted to civil rights. Not just emotional partners, the Kings were professional partners, with Coretta filling in for Martin if he was unable to make a speech or lead a rally. After he was killed, she never ceased to further their cause. Just four days after his death, she led a march of 50,000

people through the streets of Memphis, and she would continue to champion civil rights in hundreds of speeches over the next 28 years.

3. **Personal History Katharine Graham: The Story That Took Down a Presidency.** Katherine Graham also continued her husband's work after his death, but she quickly went from replacement to legend. In 1946, gender roles of the time led Graham's father Eugene Meyer to bequeath his newspaper company, *The Washington Post*, to his daughter's husband, Philip Graham. Philip Graham ran the paper for seventeen years while becoming more and more mentally unstable, ultimately committing suicide in 1963. Upon his death, Katharine didn't hesitate to take the reigns, but as the only woman publisher in such a prominent position, she had to become her own role model. Despite a direct threat from President Nixon's attorney general, in 1972 she published one of the most explosive series of stories in the history of journalism.

4. **The Year of Magical Thinking: Joan Didion: Award-Winning Analysis of Grief**

Joan Didion married writer John Gregory Dunne in the mid-1960s, just as her writing career was taking off. She would become known for her clear-eyed and shockingly honest appraisals of America, California in particular, during a time of political and social exuberance, excess, and confusion. After living and working together for 40 years, one night in 2003 after visiting their daughter in the hospital, Dunne and Didion sat down to dinner and Dunne suffered a massive heart attack and died. "Life changes in the instant. The ordinary instant," Didion writes in her 2006 memoir, The Year of Magical Thinking describing the aftermath of her husband's death.

5. A Widow's Story, Joyce Carol Oates: Prodigious Prose, Post-Loss

Joyce Carol Oates said of Didion, "Joan Didion is one of the very few writers of our time who approaches her terrible subject with absolute seriousness, with fear and humility and awe." Like Didion and Dunne, Oates and her husband, Raymond J. Smith, had a decades-long, professionally collaborative marriage. When he passed away in 2008, the once-prolific Oates was inconsolable, losing her energy for writing. After being near suicidal with grief, the intensely private Oates took on a project she had never attempted: writing about herself.

6. Jack's Widow, Jacqueline Kennedy Onassis: Generosity Abroad and in the Arts

An American icon of style and cultural refinement while her husband was alive, in 1963 Jacqueline Kennedy would become "the world's most famous widow" upon John F. Kennedy's assassination by her side in Dallas. She went on to be an ambassador for her husband's ideals, visiting Cambodia on a diplomatic mission in 1967 and overseeing the founding of the John F. Kennedy Library in Boston. Tragedy continued to plague Jackie Kennedy and her family: In 1968, her brother-in-law Robert F. Kennedy was assassinated, and in 1975, after just seven years of marriage to tycoon Aristotle Onassis, Jackie became a widow for the second time. Faced with grief that even the strongest of us might submit to, Jackie never stopped giving back.

If there was to be another widow named for "greatness" it might turn out to be someone who did a stupendous con job to escape conviction in the infamous trial for Howard Beck's killer.

In the weeks following the trial, detectives from the Police

Department, company security, and insurance investigators repeatedly combed the evidence, hoping to find something that would warrant retrying the case. Something wasn't right and they were going to find it...no matter how long it took.

In their investigations they could not find an explanation for Philip and Bill's attempt to keep Howard from exposing their hideout. They could not explain why Margaret wanted to hire a hit man to arrange Howard's death. Nor could they explain why the hit man confessed to something he didn't do.

Another mystery was the $500 check sent to Cynthia from a bank in West Virginia.

It appeared obvious that someone was trying to pin the attempted murder on Philip or Bill, or on a drunken hit man who drank his $1000 in blood money before the trial.

Investigators kept at it until police detectives and government agents working on the fraud case decided to search the cabin where Philip and Bill had been hiding. At first, everything looked normal, except there was an extra TV set in the main room, and two wash machines and two dryers in the garage. There also some extra pots and pans hanging on the walls and some file cabinets that looked oit of place.

It was intended, said the government fraud detective, that everything in the place would be confiscated as part of payback in the case.

As they examined papers in the file cabinet, they found old letters, birth and death certificates, pictures and all kinds of family records from the Townsend and Tordaloni family.

"This stuff had to be taken from the dead woman's house before police arrested them,"reasoned the insurance investigator. "Why? It's not worth much...unless," he hesitated,

"There's something in there to prove they were eligible for military benefits."

After making calls to their respective superiors, they agreed to search a little more and take the file cabinet to the police station. Evidence that could be used in a retrial of the murders, evidence of fraud and any other crimes were separated for further investigation.

The case began to unravel when they learned that Helen visited Teresa's house a few days after being told that Teresa was dead. The house was empty, windows and doors open. Police had already moved the body, which had begun to deteriorate, and the house had a terrible stench. "What happened to all her furniture?" she asked the detective.

Neighbors were asked if they saw anything going on at Philip's cabin in recent weeks. Several of the women told them about a "yard sale" being held there a couple of months ago. "It was all old stuff...but it was cheap," joked one of them.

"Who conducted the sale?" the detective asked.

"A lady in her late 50s, kind of plump...never saw her here before," answered a sweet little thing hanging on to her walker ... She was with a younger guy, also a little plump. We don't get that much traffic down here anymore."

"That doesn't sound like Margaret...did they use any names?" he asked.

"Yeah," said the little granny with the walker, "I think it was Cindy."

"What in the hell was Cynthia doing down here at a yard sale?" bellowed the officer.

"No, I said he called her Cindy," repeated the little granny.

"Thank you mom," he wisecracked...and had a whole new idea what this was all about.

The three investigators got together to discuss Cynthia's role in the case.

Cynthia married Howard Beck in 1999. He was killed in 2005. They got along for a while, had a daughter, Taylor, but she was bored ... and she wanted something better. He took out a huge life insurance policy and had a steady job at the steel mill.

Cynthia saw how Philip, and his wife and son were getting a generous income from military benefits earned by her

118

husband, John, who was killed while serving in the Vietnam War. She hatched a plan to make a bundle of money by having her husband killed in an arranged accident...and steering the blame on the Townsend's.

First, she had to convince Margaret, Philip's fashion model wife, she could get rich on a plan that involves leaving her husband, three children and ailing mother-in-law.

Cynthia offered to pay Margaret's expenses and a portion of her husband's insurance if she cooperated. Philip didn't need to know why she left. Then Philip left his mother and the kids, including Bill. Bill, who had a mental problem, was expected to take care of his grandmother and two younger sisters. Philip joined his wife in seclusion, changed their names to Tordaloni, did a number on birth and wedding names and dates...and waited to hear from Cynthia.

Margaret hired the wino from the bar to make it look like Howard had an accident. After Teresa died, Cynthia and Bill hired a truck and took everything in the house to the cabin in West Virginia. They sold almost all of Teresa's furniture in a yard sale. Bill, not realizing his mistake, counted the profit, wrote a check and sent it to Cynthia. That was her downfall.

Cynthia received a huge settlement in her suit against the company that installed the device that killed her husband, but she was not finished. Almost everyone else who had something to do with Howard's death wound up in court, charged with attempted murder. All except Cynthia were exonerated by a hung jury.

Cynthia's case was presented to a grand jury. She was indicted and tried. She got twenty years in jail.

Taylor was devastated. Her father was killed when she was only three years old. Now, her mother is going to jail. She wants to live with her grandmother, who has welcomed her with open arms. No problem.

One evening, right after dinner, the two of them watched a little TV. It was one of romantic stories where the guy gets the girl. She happens to be a widow with two children. They get married and live happily ever after.

"Gramma," Taylor mused. "if I find the right guy would you help me search his ancestry before it gets too serious?"

Helen was not amused. "I told you before...you don't pick who you want to marry...you let the guy do that...and then she threw a newspaper at her."

INDEX

ABOUT THE AUTHOR

Art Hanford Jr. has been retired since 1990 after 37 years as a photographer, reporter, managing editor, assistant editor, editor and director of internal communications for an assortment of railroads and railroad unions.

After high school in Cleveland, Ohio, he joined the Navy; graduated from the U.S. Navy School of Photography in Pensacola,FL. and served six years in the Naval Reserves.

He began his railroad career as a darkroom technician for the Chesapeake & Ohio RR in 1953, attended night school at Cleveland College, was assigned as public relations representative in '57 and hired as photograpaher-reporter for the Brotherhood of Locomotive Engineers in '58. He left the BLE in '67 and moved to Chicago to become managing editor of Railway Purchasing & Stores.

After a year in Chicago, he moved back to Cleveland as assistant editor for the Brotherhood of Railroad Trainmen, which in 1969 merged with three other rail unions to form the United Transportation Union. He served as editor of UTU News, then UTU director of internal communications until retiring on December 9, 1990.

During his career, he served one term as a councilman in Twinsburg, Ohio; had an active role in the Knights of Columbus--Garfield Hts. Council 4130; volunteered with the Universal Health Care Action Network; and served 18 years on the Garfield Hts. Board of Zoning Appeals, the last three years as chairman.

He and his wife, Janice, celebrated their 65th wedding anniversary in 2017.

They reside at the Jennings Center for Older Adults in Garfield Hts., OH. They have five children, eleven grandchildren and six (so far) great-grandchildren.

Printed in the United States
By Bookmasters